For___
Lives

Michael Flay

Polar Books

Polar Books, Koskitie 22A18 Oulu, Finland

First published by
Polar Books 1993

Made and printed in Great Britain by
Ipswich Book Company, Ipswich, Suffolk

Typeset by
CBS, Felixstowe, Suffolk

CONTENTS

THE SWISS MAN

It was plausible enough, from the outset, a fine city. To drive into the centre, along the wide roads, filled with cars, was to realise this. But a curious vacancy overhung it all, of some vague omission. For the most part you weren't aware, you went about your business, reasonable, there was no more to it than this.

The man walked down the gravelly path towards the gate. The house stood high up, on a private well kept road, with several others, overlooking the lake. This was one of the choicest areas. He was young, with a white coat and trousers, fashionable, carrying a black bag. There seemed nothing to do. So he would set out for the town, spread out below him. A pang of dissolution pushed a blankness to the forefront of his face. It seemed to him there was nothing. So he would proceed, to enjoy himself.

It was hot in the broad street where the trams ran into little bays, outside the station. The red tarmac sent up a dull, inhuman throb of heat into the baking air. Across the square the new concrete structures of a prosperous Swiss town rose unrelieved. He took his way down a side street to a small café. Sitting here, with his case, he was also plausible, a rich young man, out for a coffee and whatever else came his way. To be sure, he must have a respected job, to pay for such clothes, to have such a stance and posture. The café was crowded, dark after the white sun outside. Plumes of smoke blew upwards from cigarettes. His case was conspicuous, smart. Two girls came to his table, joked, put money on the cloth, as if in a joke. He handed them powders from his case with a smile, took the money. Others came. He sat on for a while, then left, to go to more cafés, sit and wait. It was late when he got back to his parents' villa above the lake. There was the familiar back of his fathers' car in the garage, with the wide strips of chrome each side of the number plate. They were eating together at the big oak table.

The girls could work on the powders, sit on their chairs by the typewriters, work on with a new zest and detachment. Sex too was better with these. There was a mood of running up and up onto a new level above it all, a fullness that could never be reached otherwise. Only the habit was expensive. And when the affect wore off, you were down, with the cramps running across the stomach, the trembling, and you were waiting, back in the café, for the man in white to deal you the preferred release, for which you'd do anything.

The family meal was taking place, in the long, low room with windows at the far end, overlooking the lake. The mountains closed the water round, pressing the limits of the shore back on themselves. It was enclosed and finished off. The patterned glasses were set on the blue cloth. The father sat at the head of the table, talking in German to a business colleague. The mother was in the kitchen, away. The young man sat with a glass of red wine, rocking back slightly on the chair legs, which dug into the expensive carpet.

"And you - how are you getting on?" The business colleague, deciding to be affable, turned to the younger man. "Still at the University - law, wasn't it?"

He smiled his reply. "A year to go".

"Then you can join us". The Swiss life was good, rich; you studied, then you worked, you had your material reward. By sealing up all the spaces by which dissension could creep in, the material society was secure. To speak of the point of it all was the forbidden act.

The light was fading off the lake. His mother sat by the window, smartly dressed, the appropriate object to approve, a symbol of success reached. Tomorrow she was to visit the psychiatrist again.

Up in his room he opened the case. A kind of blank exulting came over him as he stared at the wads of francs, the remaining powders. There was a pleasure to do this harm. He was past the point of caring, entered into the voluptuous slide on to the finish. If he was caught, he didn't care. And to sell, to set up deals, to ensnare: how

4

was this to be different to the rest? Rather his profiteering was more naked and truthful. His father and his associates: was what they did any different? The affect was just delayed, more indirect. Otherwise the nation of television viewers, workers, obedient endorsers wouldn't exist. He was earning for himself, doing as he'd been brought up to do.

He caught up a small polythene packet, weighed it in his hand. To put this in his head and go to town. It was one prospect rather than another. Only, why was it all so tedious?

The dark streets were thronged with young people surging about aimless, in search of some thrill. If there was nothing to aspire to except work and money making in the social credo they would aspire to those things. But en route they would have fun. To do the normal tasks in an unusual state of mind, was the new pleasure, to sip at the self-sensations.

The lake was rocking in the dark, with a wind blowing across it, from the mountains. The network of old streets would bring you sooner or later to this lake-side where couples stood against the railings and prostitutes walked. He felt again the pressure of being enclosed, surrounded by a form of life he disliked. It was to harm himself that he came here, to taste his own decline. Because, blocked, with no possibility experienced to go on, the way back was the way to take, running against the blood flow, turning all to friction and dislike.

The lamps gleamed yellow between the moving trees, which obscured then revealed the light. The thought came to him quickly, again: 'I don't like anything'. It was true, he realised If he thought it all over there was nothing he liked, neither himself or anyone - no activity. The streets were just dreary conduits to nowhere, the aims of the society were contemptible; his way of life was contemptible, in the villa. How to break out of it all?

Two people he knew vaguely were approaching to make

a deal. There were few packets left now. He was running a risk, carrying the stuff around so openly. But the packs were diminishing. He was well off, for the time being. Only the money had no interest for him. He did it all out of self despair. Quickly he slit open the remaining two packets, sniffed up the contents. He was humming now like a top. The lights were bright and cheerful, the people looking good, not the usual sick shadows. His movements were more energetic, rich. He was off, to the old suburb, with the money.

The bars were very varied. In some just young people, like students sat and drank. Others were reserved for richer clientele. In these the businessmen sat, even politicians - buying drugs with a surreptitious politeness, for their own energy and invulnerability. The world was enclosed and its people ran to invisible seed beneath the plausible appearances. Smart men in dark, expensive suits, chosen for their indication of prestige or power, did deals like the students did. It was all a hopelessness and a decay. The night passed, sitting, on the alert, with an undertow of disgust.

The car sped along the motorway, under the green signs that pointed home; the familiar names of the Swiss cities were a new nausea. Could there be an escape? The bag lay on the seat next to him. He was down on it all. His mother met him languidly as he entered the dining room. She was smart, modern seeming. Everything about her had a bought air to it. This was the impression she strove for: to have spent well, and to be seen to have done so.

"Tired?" She eyed her son. "I'll be out tonight myself." He knew her marriage wasn't satisfying to her. It was normal to have a lover, lovers, to distract herself, just as for her husband to combine a deep-snow skiing weekend with a sexual adventure. It was all distraction from the central blank.

He sat down in the familiar room as his mother moved about upstairs. All was so drearily familiar.

The next day was hot. He walked towards the town,

down a narrow path that curved round the hill, with the river below. The sun made any effort beyond the most languid, oppressive and uncomfortable. He walked hard, savouring the discomfort. The river wound back on itself, with a fast flowing current, in tight sweeps. He would head for the swimming pool, beside the river. An old creosoted fence, shabby faded cubicles made of splintered wood, stood on the edge of the river, between the pool and the water. The shabbiness was unusual in Switzerland.

He sat on a green slope, looking about. People lay on towels all around. The fence behind led to a steep wood, with the railway above. He could hear the trains run, with their suggestion of movement elsewhere. It all seemed unreal, remote: the sun on the green water of the pool, pumped out of the river weedy and slimed, the crowd of people lying there. He didn't want to stay. What exit could he strive for?

In the heat, the slope up behind the pool was a struggle. Pebbly stones cut into his feet, his arms were scratched by branches. He was up by the tracks. The silver steel stretched into a haze in the distance, the sleepers lay flat and faded. He began to walk beside the line, towards the town.

The cindery track took him down a slope towards the centre leaving the rails above. The cars moved in clusters along the wide road, leading to the centre, by the station. He felt destabilised, as if there was no purpose. He couldn't join in, or understand why he felt as he did. The futility bit into him. In spite of his neat white jacket and trousers he felt his composure slip into uncertainty. He didn't want to be a lawyer, return each night to the rich house, be part of the mechanical routine. But also, apart from this, what was there potential in himself? With a new horror, he watched the blankness unfold. Schooled to obey, to follow one image or another, to aspire as others, it seemed his initiative, his actual power to be different had collapsed, leaving an empty place where function was supposed to be. Free, he should take pleasure in the hot afternoon, he supposed, but all he felt was a vacancy, a non-response, underlain by anxiety.

In the town the composure could creep back. He could sit in a café, act normally, without being disturbed. The darkness of the inner room pleased him, as an obscuring of the outer factors. But what could he be? If his impulses outside the sanctioned aims were all broken and askance, how could he proceed?

He sat on, for the rest of the afternoon, in the half dark of the café. It was the end of the working day and the place began to fill up with those who'd been out earning the francs - necessarily, he told himself, as you need money to survive, to eat, to have a room, at the very least. Heavy men, broad and Germanic, came joylessly in, tired out. Curious: you live once, and spend much of it, your energy, on the thrust for cash. There was a bored blankness, a capacity for irritation and even violence in the spaces he confronted, acquiescence. A few younger people came in, who hadn't been to work. They also looked bored with the post drug inertia and discomfort. Could there still be a living impulse? Collectively it seemed gone.

He walked out of the café and stood in the busy square, squashed between the fashion shops, department stores and the escalators that rolled you down the subway beneath the station. People moved in close crowds, back from the work. Life went on. The impulse to more was to be kept in check til after working hours weekends. Only, if you put if off enough, the impulse will be quite killed.

Gradually the desire to go ebbed away, leaving nothing in him but acquiescence in the negation. In any case there was nowhere to aim for, nowhere to head. His volition and hope were gone, sunk away to a lower level. To resurrect them would take an impulse and motivation he could not now discover. The familiar forms of life bound him in, the symbols of daily ordinariness, the escalators, the square, the working people. Why should he be different to them?

He opened the glass door of another café, swung through

8

the thick baize curtain that was strung there to keep the heat and light out. Women sat at tables for post-work gossip; men drank coffee with small business cases open next to them. He was down and apart. In fact he knew his studies were going well, though he persisted at these with a nihilistic non-belief, as at something to be got through, a necessity. The Swiss law was tedious to him, part of the vin ordinaire he was compelled to drink whatever he did.

He sat in a corner, with a criminal look of subjection. He studied and sold the drugs in the same spirit; one thing was as good as another, all equally lifeless and tedious. He remembered having read somewhere how such feelings were those of a pure egotist. Since the society has as its core impulse that of the self-centred egotist, it's no surprise I am one. He accepted the verdict drearily, with no encroachment on his condition.

He sat on, frozen. A girl asked him for a light. He gave her one, surly and unpleasant. He wanted to flame out in negation and unpleasantness, the rottenness of the world came forth. The drugs at least constituted a world within the ordinary, made the rest bearable. Though these too, he knew, were an ultimate delusion and pain. He wanted no more to do with these. This he resolved.

It was time to drift home, be part of the tail end of the returning workers. His mother and father would be there. Although he was nearly thirty, he still lived with them, though in a self-contained flat of his own, in one wing of the villa. He could do as he chose, he was his own master. Only there were no emotions left to guide him on; all were obsolete and flat.

He'd been reading a story about a woman who broke through her jaded, finished condition by lying in the sun for months. He wondered, on the bus home, if such solutions really could work. He was too far down to make the effort of belief. All was a circle of sterility, where he could make resolutions to change that would be blown away the next minute. All his powers of volition were low and weak

9

pumping out just the strength to withstand and resist. He was like an old stoic not able to pass beyond his tolerance of negation. There was a sort of courage even in his negative withstanding; he stood his ground and faced the horrors. But the result was always a bleak goalless draw.

The bus ran round a series of curves, to lift itself from the level of the river. Railings separated the road from the drop; sign posts pointed safely at road junctions. The people sat. He wondered what kind of emotions they had as they rode along.

The walk from the stop to the house lay along a secluded road, with villas on each side, quiet and set in their own land, behind trees. There was no-one about, no community. Open garage doors showed that fathers and husbands had returned; the backs of BMWs and Mercedes, even Jaguars, stuck out of the low sunken garages, as discreet reminders of status. Inside was the coloured flicker of the television as the news was on. The trees blew gently in the warm wind from the south, from Italy. He turned up his own drive, overwhelmed with futility. Again the feeling came: 'I don't like anything, or anybody.'

Across the lake, the mountains thrust up their sterile peaks into the lower atmosphere. On these peaks nothing grew. The highest were icy with hard packed snow; on others stones baked into brittleness decomposed into the air. Below, the lake rocked in the hot wind, with no exit, no trajectory out.

He was alone, with no friend. In his accomplished, sealed off condition there was no one to touch, no one to be touched by. This too he accepted. It seemed right that it should have come to this. If nothing flowed out of or into him he could provide the quiescence required, give the kiss of acceptance to the stone-like state. Only, inside the stony covering the emotions twisted and seethed in strange combinations, colourful and lurid. Even to break a hole in the stone wouldn't be to see the emotions release in pleasured expression; still there would need some time for order and creation to be possible. His shape was bent and constricted, belying the healthy front. He knew that eventually he must attempt the release.

Now, though, there was the luridness to express. He sat up in his room like a creature in a cage, blank to emotion except a fervent anger that fed on his own suppressions. In this mood he wanted nothing. The world seemed an ape show only, in which you chose a part to follow. If you could you chose an ape-part that brought the highest returns; otherwise you were forced to act the role of the low paid ape. But, whatever level it was, it was still an ape show, without decency or justice in its overall form.

The needles and syringe, now discarded, lay in his case, with an assortment of powders. Now these things disgusted him along with the rest. A fine anger was running in him, with nowhere to gain outlet. Below the plausible surface there was the stirring and rocking of the defrauded blood. How had it come to be like this? He sat on, facing his own despair and frustration. This isolation had a voluptuous taste to it, like an evil.

For the time being he resolved to wait until the release might come. Meanwhile there had to be the stoic withstanding of the world of the ape show, the self-possession in the town centre, the hub of the ordinary life. And there was too this patient watching for the chance to split open the stone, cope with the curious forms of the sudden release. It was a mystery how it would come. But perhaps he could trust to the mystery of the flowering from an unknown source. The resistance and bitterness should not inhibit the new flow.

The evening light faded beyond the verandah that lay outside his window. He liked to stand here in the dark to feel the warmth of the impersonal wind as it blew on his face. He could hear the rustling of the waxy creepers' leaves against the smooth fabric of the house itself. The lake far below was vaguely visible in the dying night. A scent of musk from the shrubs hung in the air.

It had to be left to chance. He knew no effort of his own would break the binding his own upbringing and education, the extant world, had put upon him. Only the way out might be revealed as a sign. He could wait for the sign, and hope he would have the courage to follow it. Meanwhile he should live like an unhappy stoic.

He lay on the bed, slept.

THE SABOTEURS

She was going away, so she had to be bought new clothes, so her parents thought. The car took her down the narrow lane from the modern village towards the station, twisting across the fields that lay wet and dull on each side. The big new houses each in their separate lawned area were left behind. She saw the Persian millionairess welcoming the man in the black suit at the door as they passed. High trees formed a deep fir forest as they drove on.

She sat next to her mother, suspended. Nothing seemed quite real, yet it was all familiar. The dials of the big car, beneath the blank plastic mouldings, her mother elegant and neat at the wheel: there was a musty, stifling pitch to it all. She felt a strange revulsion rise in her, a distaste for herself in so far as she was here, doing these things.

The days had been passing quietly. She got up late in her room at the top of the house. It was large, well-furnished. Only an odd fierceness was always in her now, when she awoke. She always woke with an aversion to herself vivid in her consciousness. The day passed sitting in the room, or downstairs, her parents out. It seemed there should be more. An enormous tedium stretched out across everything. One day she had picked up a gold and silver box to keep jewels in from her father's desk. He owned a factory that made such things. He had grown rich, selling rich objects to the rich. She eyed the box curiously, turning it over in her hands. Strange, how from this came the rest - this large house, in the German village, the appearances, the manners, the objects, the way of life. The box disgusted her somehow. She was twisted in a constant vague opposition and distaste.

Her parents would send her away, to be educated. Only education to them was a case of perpetuating the appearances necessary to be social - elegance and perhaps a knowledge of a foreign language, French or English. Nothing strenuous was envisaged which might challenge the flow of rich life. And, indeed, her parents hardly saw such challenge as possible; criticism was rudeness or else misguided, therefore never to be taken seriously.

Now she was on her way to buy clothes, over the border, in the Swiss city. She explained it all to herself, literally, to counteract the unreality. 'I'm sitting in a car, I'm being taken to buy clothes'. Her mother was eccentric in spite of her neatness. She spoke in a loud domineering voice, that filled the car with heavy Germanic phrases and tones.

The train ran on across the flat, withheld landscape, towards the border. She sat looking out of the window, as her mother read a magazine. She felt numbed, as if there was no hope. The sky hung low and grey - the fields stretched out wetly towards the horizon. She was circum-vented, caught up in a restriction that had nothing to do with her. Yet her whole life had been in this richness, this world. Her mother was intact in her clothes, wearing the badge of wealthy detachment: to look at her you had to realise the world she lived in. Wherever she was, she was to be identified as belonging to the upper group, those in social command. To the girl people seemed sometimes like animals; everyone a beast in his own isolated life, grabbing as much as he could, regardless, for himself or for his family.

She pulled her fur coat round her, in a sickness. Her black hair fell onto its collar; her eyes were dark too and angry; she wanted to go into attack. The train was over the border now, running past the too clean suburbs of the Swiss city, the railway marshalling yards. She could see the names of banks lit up in fluorescent letters on buildings nearby, new shopping centres with signs in English, 'Shoppy-land.' This was the world.

Her mother stirred from her reading. There was nothing exceptional out there in the world, to recoil from. It was just a shopping trip. But the daughter was sick with a bitter kind of nausea, not to be communicated. If she could have withered the city and landscape away, she would have done it with a look.

The air was thick and heavy as they got off the train.

They walked down the long grey platform, towards the exit. To their left tall office blocks rose up, with advertisements for investment companies lit up on several. Was not this the European capital of wealth? She thought of the long line of criminals, and torturers, kings of Fascist states like the Shah of Iran, whose money lay safely here. The buildings had their roots in literal blood. Waves of tiredness seemed to come out of them, making her weak.

At the end of the platforms a dense crowd of people milled around. A few beggars moved inside it, looking for money, old men, young people in search of cash for heroin. The ragged men who lived on the station belonged to another cycle of life, invisible to her mother, except as ugliness, inconveniences. She was a mistress of never making a connexion, blind to the relations between things. This was the city of plenty, the financial centre of Europe.

The main street was clean, expensive. Trams moved silently towards the lake, past the shops. There were small boutiques for jewels and clothes. Then there were the big stores. Women in rich clothes moved in and out, sometimes escorted by wealthy men. They passed into a subway, where more goods were displayed in glass cases. The world was all goods and appearances, to be bought and sold. Her mother walked on conscious of her spending power: she could buy as she liked so she would be welcomed here. In so far as her power to spend equalled or exceeded that of the richest clients, she was of the elite. Secretly she exulted. An enormous fear in her was quelled at the realisation of her own cash safety and superiority. Without it what would she be? But she never asked the question. In the subway, worlds away from her, loitered the prostitutes and the addicts also.

The daughter allowed herself to be taken, to be bought for. She was not herself in the place she apparently occupied, but passed away into a remoter world. All the time she saw the city annihilated, wiped away. The vision of the shops, bombed out and smoking, the goods trampled into the neat paving stones, the big cars overturned, pleased her. It was also a strain, to be there and wish at the same time for this reversal. She remembered what she'd read in a book: 'never, never will they be able to share between them'. It disgusted her, the statement that the street made explicit. Nothing was shared, everything was to be snatched up, appropriated, taken away as if by rats down their individual holes. Once, a small girl, she'd seen a rat lying on its back clutching an egg it had stolen, being pulled furtively along by another rat, back to its den with the spoils. The people in the street, in blind will to have, gave her the same shudder of horror. Those who could take away the most were highest. How could it be like this? Yet thinking alone wouldn't change anything.

They walked up the fashionable Bahnhofstrasse, past the elegant jewellers, stopping to look into the windows of exclusive clothes shops. To the world it was a mother and daughter enjoying a shopping trip. There was the older woman, still attractive, smartly dressed, her clothes a badge of money and status on her. The assistants would recognise her at once as one who had the power to pay, a high member of the social stratification the shops were intended to service. And unconsciously she revelled in the knowledge that she was on top. Consciously she would deprecate. Even, she believed, it was not important to her. Yet it was her whole life.

The daughter turned with her mother across a red paved square towards one of the more distinguished department stores. Inside was a wealth of goods, set out in sections, to be bought. The mother took the girl to the clothes. The daughter was attractive herself, as she walked, a tall, proud girl, quite strong-looking with a German bigness, a 'grössenwahn' that came naturally to her. And in her silence, her refusal to be implicated in what her mother did, her passivity, the resolve formed. She would never be part of this world her mother moved in, the spirit the bright expensive city streets testified to. Her mother chattered on, and she replied as she could, on the surface. It was time to go back. She'd taken no interest in the shopping. Her mother had chosen everything. She had acquiesced, merely, for the time being, trying the clothes on, subjecting herself to her mother's fashionable scrutiny. She would like to see the packages turn to flame.

The snow fell thickly as the train moved back towards the German border. Through the window she saw the dark green landscape, covering over with white. The fields seemed inert and stolid, stupidly remote. She was lost in an anaesthetic world, obliterated. But that night her sister would be back and she could talk to her.

Her father's familiar big car stood in the drive as they approached. He sat inside his house in a high, soft chair by the fire, like a thick frog, so she imagined. The thought of how he'd spent his day, making the money, revolted her. People like him made the world. He was tired after the daily round of rich clients, expensive talk. But that night there was to be a party. The daughters were to be on show, to do him credit. She wondered how it was she had been produced here, amidst all this. The shiny rich fittings, the glass tables with chrome legs, the windows with electric blinds reflected her back at herself in a way that disgusted her. She was vile, and would remain so, in so far as she was here, she realised. And an old, long familiar sense of stifling came over her, as if she couldn't breathe anymore.

A heavy black gloom hung across the day. It seemed she liked nothing. She was always enclosed in a transparent bag, with always a fabric intervening between herself and the external world. The air seemed changed to something musty and flat by the expensive carpets, thick and muffling. She was sick at heart.

Even the carpets were symbols of oppression elsewhere. She knew how in Iran the carpet makers were forced to work for low wages, and often in bad light, so they went half-blind. And this was just so some overlord could make money, so people in Europe or the U.S.A. could possess what was regarded as a prestige object. Why not tread on people's eyes? She didn't want to think of such things. Only the take for yourself tenet was more and more hateful to her, damaging her imagination as she was forced into contact with it. What had her father ever done, except make money? Had he ever given, created? Or did he just want to suck in money, like a vacuum?

The snow fell, putting a white skin across the lawn and fields. In the distance the tall trees of the German forest rose up dark, out of the whiteness. Sometimes she walked there, with her sister. Now her black hair hung across her face as she walked with her head bent slowly round the room, with the dissolution on her. Not to be here she would transform her own consciousness, break it down. Perhaps she would take a shot of heroin, later. Or she might take the train to Hamburg, start as a prostitute. She wanted to damage herself, be impaired. She felt to blame because of her participation in this context, for the nullity that rested on her, so she wanted to find punishments to impose on her own being. She would like to cut herself about.

It was nearly dark - the white snow gleamed more, in hard crusts in the twilight. She imagined it spattered with crimson spurts of her own blood, like a king's white robe with red velvet blobs on it. As she climbed the wide, modern stairs up to her sister's room she saw her father down below watching television. Her mother was busy equipping herself for the party. It was a house of luxury and all the fittings were expensive. It reminded her, as she climbed, of a modern hearse she'd seen that morning in Zurich. How the Swiss had hated to see that shiny reminder of their own temporality in the shopping street, ignoring it as far as they could, freezing it out of their vision. She remembered the chrome shining inside the long glass window. Her imagination took her on. You opened each door in the house and a coffin stood in each room with candles round it. She saw the shops smashed, the shoppers broken open like dummies, lying on the pavements. How to let in the life she strove for?

Her older sister was lying on the bed, smoking a cigarette. She also had long black hair, sharp insolent features, eyes that held you for a while in fixed, assessing gaze and then usually dropped away in dismissal, if you didn't correspond to what she required. She was by herself, in general.

"Why is it all so useless?" the younger girl asked. "It seems to come out of the houses. The money sends it out, something to kill off your impulses. It makes me sick". She answered her own question.

The older girl moved silently to the window, opened it, stood looking out into the darkness. A shaft of sharp, frozen air blew in. She spoke in self-parody: "We must bring in something else, not required here". The two girls began to get ready.

The family sat in the large downstairs room, to receive the guests. The whole scene struck the girl as a delirium: anything might happen it was so unreal. Yet she knew too that her mother saw it all as a final reality. There was no going beyond or superseding the established forms allowed. The other guests would all be rich too. The world was sealed in, but its sick influence spread out, like poison leaking from a canister. These were the successful of Germany. The little village was a refuge of the rich, a sanctuary where their lives could be led out. They could be unseen here, each endorsing each other's way of life, seeing no questions and asking none.

"You must look pretty for the visitors." The mother looked her daughters over with pride. Externally they might look the part now. But she had no legislature over what they felt, no real idea of what they thought. She sensed a veiled resistance in them, that was all. And, in any case, so long as they went through the motions with apparent enthusiasm, particularly attending to their appearance, what did their emotions matter? The mother looked round at the rich room, the emblems of achievement. It was all there, like a room in an advertisement for prestige goods. So the achievement was sanctioned, endorsed, and proved by the objects, the house itself. As for the rest, it seemed to her there was nothing. Why speculate further than you need, make yourself unpopular and uncomfortable?

In spite of the snow the guests were punctual. Business men living locally, their wives, came through into the spacious hall-way to be welcomed. No-one was there out of genuine friendship. It was a meeting to endorse mutually, perhaps to make or enhance a useful financial contact. The black limousine of the American Ambassador could be seen turning into the curved driveway. This was a personal friend of the father - in so far as friends were possible in a world based on taking, maximising one's own position at any cost, the mania to have and have again. There was a flurry of suited men shaking hands, women in expensive dresses exchanging banalities.

The new conservative worlds of the States and Germany were endorsed with smiles - there had just been elections. Everything was for the best now. The drinks were handed out. The room was full of men in suits and ties, wives, and a few grown up children who were running smoothly in their parents' narrow tracks. It was like an advertisement for a prosperous and happy society; the bright rich dresses of the women, the immaculate men. How could there be anything else? The younger sister stood on the margins, watching. It was like a television show. The presence of the American and his entourage increased this sense - one of those American status business dramas where everyone is out to destroy the other, rise up, and the women are all beautiful and fine on the surface. The people lived down at this level, each in a fine house, finely transported, insulated.

The Ambassador moved across to talk to the younger daughter. The room was crowded with groups of people chatting, drinking. In his white suit and blue tie, his habit of smiling and easy talk, he felt himself to be set off well,

22

like a character on television. The girl attracted him. He knew he was the highest status person present.

"You should see L.A. in the summer. It's simply gorgeous. If you'd like to stay with us, then you're welcome."

"Why should I want to stay with you?"

She turned and walked back to near where her sister was trapped in conversation with a director of a Swiss chemical company. The company liked to test out new products under the guise of 'helping' developing countries. Sometimes the patients helped in such a way developed disturbing symptoms as a result of these experiments.

The Director was also in search of some easy erotic reward. It was as if the socially regarded success had in some way twisted the brains of these men, so they really believed everyone must respect and admire them. Only misfits or jealous people would interpret them as negligible or perverted. His face creased into an easy smile, the smile of a spokesman before the television cameras reassuring viewers that the malicious reports they'd heard elsewhere were quite without basis. His expensive ease was generally found to be reassuring.

The elder sister was letting him talk, listening to see how he'd reveal himself. She pretended to be pleased at the recent election success of the right.

"So, I said to the Minister, it is important not to discredit the Nazis entirely. After all, they wanted just the glory of Germany. Each nation wants glory: look at Britain, so admirable in the Falklands".

The sister eyed him indifferently. He stood there in his suit, with one arm bent to hold his drink in its rich crystal glass, plausible. Anyone who saw him might imagine him to be a good fellow, in spite of his views. And he was useful to his company precisely for his plausibility, his capacity to put across unjust views and give them credibility by his manners, to disguise self-interest and callousness as common sense.

"You think you're a big person, don't you?"

23

He looked at her complacently. He liked a challenge.

"I have succeeded, yes".

"But your success puts others off succeeding".

She moved away, leaving him by the tables of drinks, the silver dishes with elegant snacks. He shrugged, began to talk to his neighbour. He was indifferent to her opinion. Plenty of women would be pleased to agree with him, liaise with him, enjoy the comforts and insulations he could buy them. And it was in general a thrill for a woman to be with a big important man. It was genetic, natural, he believed, part of the survival of the fittest and best. That he was of the best, the highest evolved alive then, he had no doubt.

The girl turned to her younger sister. "Let's go, do what we planned". No-one would be very surprised at their departure. And in any case everyone was too involved in talking and drinking to notice what they did.

The door swung closed and they were out in the cold sharp air, moving towards the fir trees. They stretched in for miles, dark tall trees with white below, in patches, frozen hard. But between the trees and the girls was about half a mile of fields, covered in snow.

The snow was crisp and firm as they trod into it moving always further away from the suburb of rich houses. They were walking along the path towards the forest and the houses were dwindling to nothing behind them, swallowed up in the night's blackness, devoured. Only the yellow street lights, if they turned, gleamed dirtily out onto the snow. Above them a small curved moon hung over the trees. There was a new impulse in them, to let in some new energy. The girls swayed in and out of the trees, in their thick coats; with snow in their hair that hung frozen in little beads, lit up in the moonlight, like white shiny traceries in the black. They were sisters, on their way.

Suddenly the house loomed up, in a wide clearing, like a park. The snow lay untouched over the lawns, gleaming fresh and pure in the darkness. An American flag hung

24

lifeless on a pole in front of the main entrance. This was where the ambassador lived. The house was white also, impure against the snow. It had a costly, weighty, unpleasant look, cumbersome there among the trees.

Only a few lights were on, in the servant's quarters. You could see the girls go on, in their brown fur coats, between the trees, then on up the drive, towards the front door. They had often been here before, to visit the ambassador's own daughters. But now his family was in the States, and he lived here alone, with a housekeeper. It was his country residence. He had a larger house in the city.

The girls paused to ring the bell. The housekeeper know them. She also knew the ambassador liked the company of young women.

"We've come to wait for him. He asked us to. We wanted to walk in the snow".

The housekeeper showed the girls up the staircase to the daughter's rooms and left them there. The staircase was substantial and sweeping, with a broad red carpet, white banisters, appropriately imperial.

"What shit!" The elder sister turned to the younger girl, smiling. Her black hair curled to her shoulders, she moved gracefully. The objects appropriate to a young, expensive life decorated the room, electrical equipment, luxurious but casual furniture, expensive wardrobes for clothes.

"And he wanted us to go to Los Angeles with him! Have sex with him. He'd have to take that cream suit off first. And those shoes! He wouldn't exist then". The younger girl began to laugh as she spoke, in mockery. She walked stiffened, in a parody of his rich conceit, across the carpet.

"If he came back now he'd think we wanted him".

Out of the window she could see the snow still falling hard across the darkness. The whole ethos was sick. It wasn't just the ambassador. The established world of money makers, politicians, the upper strand, was vile to her. She felt a strong anger rising.

The girls moved cautiously now, up a further flight of

stairs, towards the loft. You could fold down a ladder, and climb up into the roof itself. The bare rafters leaned in raw diagonals all around, the wood flaky and exposed. The older sister pulled out a can from her large overnight bag and began to pour its contents over the bare beams. Her black hair still caught particles of snow which gleamed there in bright vivid spots, as she worked. Her hair was deeply black, with a shiny richness, like an animal's fur, a well-kept Persian cat. The younger girl struck a match and dropped it in a small pool of petrol. Soon a steady flame was burning all across the soaked rafters.

Quickly they climbed back down the ladder, sealing the heavy trap door of the loft behind them. For a while the fire would burn up there unnoticed. The girls passed back down the stairs, out of a side door. In the dark they crossed the white lawns towards the forest. Already through the night you saw the fierce orange light of the blaze, visible in the attic windows. But as yet nothing would be evident, either below, or from the village. The destructive blaze was sealed in, out of sight, like a more or less invisible disorder, behind a gracious frontage.

The girls turned to watch the glow. It was a release, to stand there in the sharp cold air and see the expensive house secretly burning, the destruction contained inside. But soon it would break out, and be plain to everyone. The start of the revenge they craved, for the days of repression, for the self-centred life of their parents and their associates, for the selfish social norms, was there taking form before their eyes. It was a start. The accumulated poison was to be destroyed.

They reached a road, stretching bleak and icy, empty in both directions. They would meet their friends, a few miles further on, as planned, drive to the city, get away, plan the next move, the next target.

THE PLAYER

That was his pleasure - to hit the ball hard and low, there across the dirty green grass. The blocks were all around. But he wasn't conscious of them. The white ball spun like a blur, between the posts. He ran to retrieve it, the breath tangling in the misty evening air. The motorway ran alongside, elevated, a constant of noise. He saw his mother high up, on the concrete balcony. Then he was back, alone, with the ball. Again and again he would send it curving across the spaces of the pitch. He never thought what it meant. Only it was a freedom to be there, oblivious.

One evening he noticed the small man, watching. He stood huddled up in an old coat, with a wizened face, like a small monkey, quiet there, under the flats. He ignored him. A few of the boys were knocking the ball back and forwards; you heard the smack of the foot against the plastic, saw the air curling in the cool night, lit up by the motorway lights above. The white ball spun between them, meaningless. They were involved, given up to the movement, in motion. The monkey-man lit a cigarette, watched them for a while.

They were off the pitch now, walking up the gravel path, towards the blocks. The boy didn't speak; the others left him alone. His eyes had a slightly dazed look, as if he couldn't understand. There were the flats, rising up out of the land, like something rotten stuck in the ground. But he had no means to compare them with anything different. He drifted, like in a sleep, up the path. Then he saw the monkey-man up ahead, like a figure in a story he'd been read once. That was how it seemed, like a myth come real.

"You like to play a bit then?" The man looked at him, sideways. The boy didn't speak, walked on, in a mirage. "Like to play?" The man repeated the question. The boy looked back at him, startled out of his trance. He stared at the man, walked on. The man smiled, stood back.

The bell rang in the flat. The woman was washing up the plates with the TV on. The boy sat on the settee, watching the images. It was the man; he stood there, sly and

29

determined.

"Is that your boy?" The woman was startled, defensive.

"What if it is?"

"Send him along, on Friday night. Up to the ground."

She stared at him, sullen.

"You'll send him, then?"

She shut the door, firmly. The boy had heard it. The mother ignored him, went back to wash the meal plates.

It was cold and wet at the bus stop. A sharp wind blew across the squares of grass and cut into the few people waiting. He stood withheld, holding his bag. In his mind he saw nothing. He just felt the rain and wind tear at him, smelt the air heavy with fumes around him, heard the traffic on the motorway. He was always cut off, suspecting a blow withheld. His mother was a blank in his mind, something he never thought of. Only a pain was in him he didn't consciously know was there. He looked at the grass lit up under the street lights and at the white posts gleaming in the half-dark. It was a total other world where he could move, in contained rules and order, but free inside these.

The lights were on at the ground. The grass was lurid, beneath them, pure and extensive. A kind of sharp excitement ran in him, at the sight. He'd seen the side play, on television. He'd never come. He couldn't connect himself with a team. Even when he played, he was a phenomenon that moved among other phenomenon, connected by the flying curve of the ball, the vicious hard trajectory of the volley - the players like birds wheeling in a pattern in a deserted landscape, all silently connected up. He didn't exist - another force did. It was like a poem, the game: it didn't exist because of the players. They were secondary. A force flowed into them from outside. He couldn't see it as tables, results. He was a young priest of the flow of the ball, silently and sensually initiated into its movement.

The dingy door led into a courtyard, with black cinders across it. He saw the big cars lined up, in the park. The manager would be there, to watch, he supposed. Inside the changing room, other new players, here for the trial, were putting on their boots. He went quietly and sat in a corner of the room. The others looked at him quizzically - he looked back at them, nervous. A few were making jokes. But they were all agitated.

The short man was talking tactics to them. He seemed more dominant here. Before he had been unobtrusive, faded into the evening, near the flats. This was his context, his area of work. You could tell it was his whole life by the gleam in his eye. The words he was using meant nothing - they just were vehicles for the under emotion. It was the game that counted. And the game was meaningless, gratuitous. What could have less point? But everyone was there united for the pointless thing.

A few of the regular players were there too. These new youngsters had been watched for weeks. Some would definitely be chosen tonight. The older players would also have a say in the selection. Vaguely he recognised faces. That one - he'd been a defender when they played that German side. Another face he remembered from the television. He was getting excited. Could he be like these? But off the pitch these men looked suspended, as if they had no real existence. In their club blazers they looked absurd, cheated of something. There was a weighty, hulking aspect to them - men at a loss. Yet they were famous, rich. So why did they have no meaning? They didn't seem to know what to do. It was only when the boys ran out onto the lurid grass that they came alive.

He was playing, in a dream. There were no conceptions in his mind. All was a blank, except for the bursting of energy through his body, the rain on his shirt, and the ball. The ball was the centre, the pivot of the world. He was given up to its demands. He was drawn instinctively to be shadowy, to drift in almost unobserved, lean round his opponents, like one asleep, with the ball there at his feet, drift and drift. And then came the superb violence, the smack of the ball so sharp and hard, the projectile rushing towards the white posts, luminous under the flood-lights. He was playing well, in the trance of possession.

They wanted him, after the game. So this was to be his life, here. He would arrive, tread across the cinder path, move with the other players in the ritual of the training. He couldn't imagine them very clearly. He wouldn't make any conscious ideas up about them. He liked to leave it all vague, so he could act in the shadows, with the veil round him. His instinct was not to be approached, to keep remote.

He lived in the flat with his mother. She hardly spoke to him. Her husband had left her with the young child. A frustrated bitterness seized her up. She hated the child, as something she was responsible for. So her lips would twist in deformed insult. "You're a rat," she would tell him, "A little sick rat." So the boy was used to blows, a sickness in the world, quite early.

Now he stayed on there, silent. The mother would watch television, sitting hulked in front of the set. He sat in an abstracted world, where he was neither thinking nor day dreaming. He couldn't make concepts. He just knew when he was hurt, in a dumbness.

The football was all he had. Each day he set off for the ground, waiting at the bus stop with the rest. He hardly noticed anyone. Other people were there, like boulders in the landscape. He never approached anyone. He had no friends. Only on the field did he burst into expression. The pent-up, focused outflow of energy and self-giving, took place just there. The other players didn't understand his silence. But, because he played so skilfully, beyond them, they acknowledged him, admitted him as one of them.

It was a wet morning. The players were training. Round the edge of the ground the old stands rose up, skeletons, rusty, like shadows. The boy was with the reserves. As he rose up and down, pressing his body to the damp ground, lifting it up, on and on in a mindless rhythm of contact, a man came into the shadowy stand above him. He was almost invisible, like a ghost. A light plume of smoke rose from a cigarette in his hand, rising up as vapour, in the rain. The practice game began. It was dark, the morning heavy with thunder. The boy was running across the blackened grass, his boots thudding into the wet surface, curving the ball this way and that. The other players were tricked by him again and again. His body swung and feinted, lifted into action, expression. The ball spun across to him and he touched it hard to the player running to his left, then watched the white circle splatter between the posts. There was a voluptuous satisfaction to feel the ball move like this, beyond sexuality. The man in the stand looked down. The ball was again with the boy. He was running, then with a twist passed the two players ahead of him, curving the ball again precisely to the posts. He liked to curve the ball in a weird flow. The game ended.

The other players eyed him, with a respect he didn't at first recognise. He always left the field dazed, exhausted, with even his vision blurred. "You'll be in the first team, if you go on like that." He didn't know what words to use. It was as if the frame-works required were all too small for him so he couldn't communicate. He worked in a different way to most people. "Why don't you come with us tonight? To the disco." He shook his head. The others let him alone.

The next week he was in the first team. The manager had watched him often enough to risk the experiment, which was a success. Each week he played in a kind of abstracted, intense possession. He was even a star. The papers wrote about him. But still he lived on with his mother, in the flat.

The players tried to get him to go with them. One night they succeeded. He didn't know why but he found himself giving into their requests. Why shouldn't he join in? Something stirred in his brain. He would try it out. Normally so withheld, moving backwards and forwards between the flat

and the ground, sitting in his trance in the flat while his
mother watched television, he would draw on out, alter the
pattern. He hardly knew what he was doing. He only found
expression there on the pitch. Women for him hardly existed. There was a remoteness round him that he maintained as an instinctive protection. He always wanted to
keep his distance, as if there was a threat implicit in each
approach. In a way it seemed as if the very power of his
play depended on his isolation, the maintenance alone of
his integrity. Perhaps his nature was finer than the rest, or
recognised instinctively its own special reality. For who
could he have related to? He was like a priest to his own
mystery and gift, knowing no-one else could approach the
power he was in contact with. To be with ordinary people
was to feel alone, because of the gap between his knowledge and theirs. And no communication would bridge the
gap. It was a question of instinctive knowledge and refine-
ment. Only tonight he would go with them.

The streets were wet as usual, and the cars moved slow
below the coloured lights of the clubs and bars. The players were excited, watching the women on the pavements,
looking forward to the night ahead. They straggled in
through the entrance. The manager of the nightclub came
forward, obsequious. He'd been told in advance the players
were coming. They were among the top teams in England;
some of the players were internationals. There would be a
show, then a disco. The players were in a buzz of triumph,
high spirited. "Yeah, we did all right today, then. Didn't
we?" The show manager grinned, slightly wary. What if
they got out of hand? "Yes lads, a good one today. Three-
nil." He waved his hand to beckon them in, the fingers
stained with nicotine, the rings flashing on the fleshy main
fingers under the dim coloured lights. "We've some friends
here for you tonight."

The players sat down in a little darkened room like a
theatre. Red velvet curtains hung across in front of a small

34

stage. The young player felt a tug of surprise. What was to come? The footballers were the only people in the room. Strange electric music played. From somewhere bottles of whisky were produced, left out under the chairs by a thoughtful management, no doubt. The stars unscrewed the bottles, began to drink. "Come on, try it." The international forward opened the young player's bottle, held it to him. "Come on, you've made it. Make the most of it." He liked the lad, wanted him to open out a bit. "Why not?" The boy drank. He liked it here with the men. Why had he held back? Something unfroze in him. He would try it all out.

It was still quite early. The players knew vaguely what was to come. To the boy it was a type of mystery. He was still virginal. Women seemed not really to exist for him. But he was curious. It seemed the barriers were breaking.

The lights went lower, suddenly. The red velvet curtain parted and a weirdly dressed man came through the gap. He wore dark glasses and a multi-coloured shirt, with black leather trousers and a black cape. He was consulting his watch, tapping with a gold stick on the ground. The curtain opened wider to show a house built of flimsy canvas. All the time an insistent, electric piece of instrumental music played. The man turned idly to look at the upper window of the house. The players were quiet now, absorbed in the mime. Suddenly the left half of the upper storey peeled away to reveal a woman sitting on a chair. It was an old wooden chair, reminding the player of the chair he'd sat on at school. The man with the cape watched her, apparently half-bored. She carried on as if no-one were there. She wore a tight black skirt with a slit in the side, a neat white blouse, high heeled shoes. She was perhaps just back from the office. The players were intrigued by the drama. The man pointed with his stick. She began to unbutton the blouse.

The young player watched. All his latent sexuality began to arouse. She leaned over the edge of the frame of the top part of the house, hanging her breasts down. The man

35

opened the door, went in. Slowly he unzipped the skirt, pulled off his own trousers. She began to move her fingers up and down on his tight shaft, move herself towards him. The young player watched, fascinated. All his physical energy rose up in him. The atmosphere was genial, as the players watched. Their appetites were being sharpened.

Another section of the house was folded back. On the top level, at the right, a black girl, like a student, in jeans and pullover, sat at a desk. She was reading. Suddenly she yawned, paused for a while, staring into space. She began to take off her pullover languidly, then to undo her jeans. From the background came into view a tall negro. He came forward slowly, unzipping his trousers as he advanced. She was shocked at first, then accepted. It was all impersonal.

The music played louder, and wafts of grey smoke rose up in the dark room. The young player was half drunk with the whisky, caught up in the unfamiliar atmosphere. He wasn't shocked. It was like a revelation. The other players sat relaxed and watching. They were like warriors, full with physical efforts made, their bodies real and potent. What did it matter that it was all impersonal? Who really cared? There was an impersonal need in the men to express their sexuality, as there was in the women. But so far it was to be visual, merely.

The turn was over. There was a faint burst of applause. The music changed, even more electric and ethereal, abstract. The players exchanged glances, sat in the chairs, affected by the alcohol, the show itself. The young player was intent, wandering what would happen next. For the time being, no-one spoke. The game had been a hard one, the goals coming in the last fifteen minutes. They were tired. But in any case, there usually wasn't much talk between them.

A velvet covered door opened at the back of the room, beyond the stage, and the girls who had been performing came out, dressed as they had been before. Behind them came the negro and the man in the multicoloured shirt with little mirrors sewn into it, more girls in brightly coloured skirts and shoes. A strange white vapour began to stream round the door also, like on an old-fashioned television show when a ballad singer sings. "We've got a surprise for you" the man in the shirt said. "He's been a fan or yours for a long time. He's got some friends with him....!" Round the corner another curtain parted. Here were banks of electrical equipment, amplifiers, lights. Guitars lay up against them. Then faces the players recognised emerged dimly from a back room. The musicians strolled up to the instruments. The lights went down again, and new multi-coloured beams, red, green, blue picked out the band. The women moved to sit among the players. By now a few other guests had filtered in, friends of the band, of the players. The music began, swelling up and up to a new volume of rhythm and loudness. It was hard, physical. The room was suffused in smoke, lights, whisky and a kind of quiescent silence, physical too, in the audience. Everyone was getting lost in the sound and the atmosphere. By now the young player was lapsed out too, into a relaxed ease. One of the girls was lying against him, her legs slightly apart, in a black skirt that fitted tightly to just below her knees. Her blouse was full, and he could feel the pressure of her breast as she lay against him. She was warm, lying there, in a kind of blur, as the drummer smashed out, at the drums, given up to the music, and the guitarists leaned together, in the hazy room, oblivious, while the blue lights lit up the red bodies of the guitars. Other women were with the other players.

The band played on and on. The time passed. The room, always dim, was filled with bodies lying in weird positions, the clothes of the women dishevelled, the men hot and eager. After a while the flesh itself lit up under the lights - everyone was undulating back and forth, impersonal. Why not like this? Hadn't it always taken place in the past, the reward of the victors? And even the compensation for the losers. To bury oneself in the flesh, to exist, just as a body, to be oblivious.

The young player was in a side room with the girl. He was carried away in the intoxication of it all. He was not himself. He could not see the girl. Only he wanted to respond to her, to give himself up. He was tired with the stress of his constant reserve, the withholding that was his habit. The girl was controlled, aware of what she was doing. The motions were familiar and easy. Nothing was at stake. Was it a pleasure? There were no more issues. She looked at the man, who was lapsed out in the new sensations of the evening, could see he was handsome. He was just male to her, no more. He could see dark hair, a body, the rest unknown. She began to feed him into herself with a curious greed. It was a pleasure to feel the young flesh sink into her, almost a triumph. She would move and twist. Outside the band played on still; through the closed door she heard it. The man was given up, oblivious almost. His face was losing its boyish clarity, and gleam, as a tiredness of sensation crept across it. He was finished soon, in the queer oblivion. She crouched back.

Each time she took a man it was as if she asserted herself supreme over him, made him less than herself. He must gratify her. She must have her experience. She must force him to please her. And then, the experience over, she was replete for the while, until the next time. It was a mania, to be beyond emotion. To became the female incarnate, to be subserved, to snatch it up. She always felt more separate after the experience, more immune and sealed off than ever, remote from any connexion with the man. She looked down at the youth with a thrill of victory, something gained. His eyes were closed now, and he breathed steadily, the fine hair like a child's across his forehead, the deep chest moving gently. She got up casually to open the door. Another girl was coming in. Blue smoke from cigarettes was lit up briefly, visible through the half-opened door, then vanished. Waves of music blew in, the laughter of the other players, voices.

38

The new girl was flushed slightly, with the efforts. In her too was the curious gleam of female vindictiveness, the desire to do harm. It was a triumph to take the men, to feel they wanted her, while she gave nothing back. Curious how in the act of sex itself the attitude of the girls crystallized out, most polarised, as a subtle antagonism, hatred of the male. And in the desire to extract the maximum sensation, as in a chemical retort, was the hatred. They wanted to be immune, beyond contact. The gratification was to be theirs alone.

The night was drawing to its close. The young man lay in an uncomfortable sleep in the side room. The players came to look for him, wake him up. The international forward pulled him to his feet. He was in a stupor. The older player grinned, supported him with his arm. "You've really made it, kid. This is it." But the youth heard nothing. He was stupefied. They moved out to the cars, into the cool air of the morning. Rubbish was piled up outside the clubs; a few cars were moving. It was another world out here, in the dawn.

He woke up in the flat with the daylight shining in through the window. Vaguely he tried to remember. His mother was clattering with the plates in the kitchen. He heard the television on in the background. A curious depression hung in his body. Yet, in his mind, he was pleased to have known the woman. Only his blood ran slow and thick now. "It was the drinks", he told himself. And he got up to wash, cover himself with water. There was no training that day. Perhaps she would see him later. He could get the number from the directory. He felt the impulse to open out to the girl, to follow something through with her. He ignored the anxiety in his blood. He was anxious because he wanted her, that was all. There was a new need in him.

He was looking forward to making the call, to hearing her. All day he sat around, vaguely waiting. At last he was dialling the number. He was put through to her. He could hear vague noises of clearing up in the background. "Maybe we could meet sometime?" he was asking her. "Well I'm busy, and what for anyway?" Her voice was cold, withheld. What did he think he was doing, confusing things this way? He felt his heart go icy. "Oh, nothing." He put the phone down in a blank anger. She had just taken him for nothing. He felt abused, cheated. So he was learning, now, what it was like in the outer world.

He went out into the street. The estate was weakly lit up by the concrete lamps, curving over at the top, and a light fog gave each shining light a rainbow halo, eerie. There was no-one about. The area was completely blank. What should he do? There seemed nothing. The next training was tomorrow. Some new impulse was awake in him now, a need to connect up with something, someone, share himself. But instead, a kind of insulated, remoter self was forced on him. There was nothing to connect up to. Inside the flats sat people, some in relation with others. He was outside. A few boys were kicking the ball about on the road. He stood and watched. They didn't recognise him as the player; he stood, obliterated, not wanting to be seen, with a sadness, a physical lethargy, filling him up.

He walked for an hour, pressing on through the streets, towards the club. The shop windows were lit up, and a few people wandered aimlessly about the cold centre, looking in at the goods on display. It would soon be Christmas. Perhaps he should kill the girl. The thought came to him as he walked the empty street. A hot impulse to kill her filled his veins. He would go, wait for her to come out, kill her for the injustice. But a warning impulse also urged him not to give himself away again. He just had to accept the damage. It was strange, how he felt it physically, like a new tiredness injected into the blood. Nonetheless, a morbid curiosity drew him to the club again. Along the street were parked the big cars of the clients, come to be gratified. He felt suddenly weakened, as if something sick was against him. Why did he come here? He stood in a doorway watching. Something sensitive in him was violated, making him angry. He was turned back on himself as usual. He thought of the game. There were the lights, burning white in the dark, wintry afternoon, the grass illuminated, bright green, the red shirts of the players. He saw himself, given up to the game, running, twisting, the fierce volley of the ball. It was only there he was anything. Now the realisation made him feel desperate. He didn't want to be so cut off. And he felt no real involvement in the team, in the league tables. He didn't care. Only he must give himself this expression. He could only communicate there. He was damned up, beyond communication with anyone. Only now even this power seemed to have an ashiness to it. He wanted the girl. She had taken him, so why didn't she want him now? He knew too he was being naive. Life was life, you have to take the knocks. Only there was something degrading, ignoble about taking them. It was humiliating to be with other people. He didn't want to adapt to what they were, what they did.

He watched the door open, the girl came out. She was wearing a white coat, quite smart. Her brown hair hung over the collar. She looked plausible, not hungry. She had used him to snatch her own invulnerability from him. So, in sex, she reached a position of strength for herself, and only for herself. She wanted to be immune. It was her mania. Now she looked even gentle, submissive. There was a man beside her, tall, in a long brown well-tailored overcoat. He carried an attaché case. All his movements, trappings, suggested total social adaptation, the confidence of acquiescence. She had her hand on his arm, was looking up at him attentive, respectfully tender. He watched from the shop entry, faintly nauseated. And he was confused. Was she in fact capable of being tender? He was half-tempted to believe she was. But then he remembered her own behaviour to him. She was cancelled out for him now. He had learned. All he felt was a kind of blankness, not even anger, the need to harden his own being. The car

41

door slammed, the woman was inside, to be taken away to some apartment: another life.

He walked back through the dirty streets of the town. The concrete shopping precinct was curiously desolate, in the cold night air. Before, he would have drifted through, blind. Now, because he wanted to join up, he noticed the loneliness of it all. He was the only person there now. The dummies in the shop windows looked back at him, draped with clothes, elegance. What connexion was there between himself and all this? A whole flood of emotion was pouring into him now. He wanted to be hard. He would grind her out of his brain, together with the images of the town. But occasionally came the flashes of revenge, the desire to harm what had harmed him.

The lights were on as the players ran out onto the pitch. A great cry like the moaning of beasts went up, round the ground. The team was almost at the top of the division now. And tonight they were playing a foreign side in a European game. The young player was oblivious, his anger sharpening his desire to begin, a fury focused in the desire to overcome, to defeat. The crowd was shouting vaguely in the distance. He noticed the curious faces of the foreign players, their different bodies, thinner, apparently more athletic than the English players. He received the ball, began to run, sliding it sideways, back again to the international forward. The ball came back to him, and he knew he would force it in a vicious curve, to defeat the rest. The white ball spun cruelly towards the posts, bending out the net as it hit it hard. The foreign players eyed him warily now. The game went on, catching him up in its rhythm. He was surrendered to it totally, the anger giving him more speed, more ruthlessness. He hit the ball across from the wing, low and deadly. The midfield player ran to hit it in. The crowd were moaning in a pleasure in the background. The player didn't hear them. He would have his revenge on the girl in his own submission to his art. The

42

foreigners were uneasy now, arguing among themselves. A kind of hatred seemed to swell up in their eyes.

It was the second half. The ball came to him again on the right wing. He ran with it, passed to the big mid-field player, ran on. He got the ball back, hit it brutally towards the goal. He was flowing now, impersonal, given up to the force. Serving his own religion, he had a completeness that was beyond relation. He couldn't share this art with anyone. So what had he to give to a woman? She must be cut off always from his most vital function and fulfilment.

The game was more or less over. The foreigners were arguing still as the whistle blew. The young player was redeemed in his own eyes. He walked off the pitch in his usual daze of exhaustion, so tired even his vision blurred. A few of the other players grinned at him. He was beyond them too. Only he felt gratitude to them, a silent connexion in the blood with the men. There was no need to speak.

In the changing room the curious depression came over him again. There was nothing else now to go to, nothing further to have. No woman was waiting for him. He had given himself all out. Now he wanted some return, something given to him. Who would give him something? A strange residue of resentment welled up, as if he did everything for nothing. Who would want him, really want him?

It was the further need that dominated him now, to find the counterpart for his efforts. He didn't want to stay alone. But the paradox was, the greater the efforts made, the greater the need. He sat alone in the flat, with the new stress on him.

THE PERSIAN DAUGHTER

She was sitting bored, in the flat. It was her usual state. The room was small and square; the electric fire filled it with thick heat. Her family's house, back in Teheran, was large and spacious. So this cheaper living was novel to her, deliberately chosen. She had no thoughts as she sat. Instead a number of fixed prejudices and attitudes circulated in various combinations in her slow mind. Purer impulses were trapped up and distorted in this mental frame.

She was turning over an impulse, "I want to love, to be loved". Only the Persian idea of love acted as an inhibition on her, stopping her move. She should desire absolutely, not eat or sleep for love. The man should do the same. Then he should serve her absolutely, in service of her supreme beauty. She should command him. She had been brought up on this idea. Meanwhile, in the absence of such a reality, she was bored.

She moved nervously, towards the window. She was a large girl, sensual looking; her heavy breasts sagged below her pullover. Her body moved heavily, as if nothing lit it up. The street was blank, suburban, a main road ran past a corner shop. There was a weight on her. She unscrewed a jar by her bed and swallowed a tranquilliser. It was a habit. She looked at the clock. The man she lived with wouldn't be back for two hours. What should she do? She was at a total loss. There was nothing she could do. She lay down on the bed.

The process that had brought her this far had begun long ago. No-one had thought to teach her anything that might develop her feelings or her thoughts. Rather they spun in her in chaos, unevolved and unquestioned. "Black people were dirty". "Other people were low class". Yet inside her scheme of prejudice she could be kind, generous.

She lifted the phone. The number rang out in Teheran. Her parents were speaking to her. They sent her money to live. They had educated her, as they thought, sent her to beauty schools, and to learn languages. Her mother had

47

married at 15. The daughter would be married. Meanwhile it didn't matter what she did. She herself was a child of the Shah's society, brought up in material lavishness, and indulgence. She was the lucky one, to be pampered. "The men should pamper the women". This was one of her tenets. She spoke dreamily in a drugged voice to her mother, reassured to hear her. Her parents could buy her out of any difficulty, she knew. The call was all family gossip.

Finished, she wondered what else she might do. Her whole body was numb, in any case. The drug made her damp, lethargic. She just sat, waiting.

Downstairs the door clicked open. Two men followed each other, running up the stairs. Both were quite short, one slim, the other rather stout and self-important. She lived with the slim one. Here was amusement for her. The other sold drugs at the university, had richer parents; life was for pleasure. Although the girl lived with a man, she was still a virgin. She felt a curious pull, toward the dissolute one. It was in her nature to be drawn to the illicit and the furtive. What was good and pleasurable took place in devious and hidden ways. The little man eyed her. She liked his sharp features, like a rat's, shying away yet defiant, and the way his chest stuck out. He was on a small scale, like a model of someone else. He would flatter her deliberately. Then perhaps he could sleep with her. Then he would throw her away, maybe blackmail her. It would be a serious matter in Iran. He was calculating.

They all sat in the kitchen. "Go - make some tea". The woman took revenge on the slim man. She would dominate him. He didn't satisfy her, yet she lacked the will or confidence to separate. So she would torture him too. The man moved to do as she asked. Besides, if he loved her, he should do all she wanted even if it was to humiliate him, even if he knew she was wrong. If he argued with her, she would sulk and shout against him. This was the typical Persian female game, to brook no argument. Either the man accepted what she wanted or should go elsewhere.

As for reaching down to any real wants, how could she do that? Everything was masked, wrapped up in social or religious form, known in advance, pre-set. The mask was never off. To love someone - didn't she know in advance what she was meant to feel? And certainly she had never stayed awake all night for the slim man. It was proved, then - she didn't love him.

A kind of negative power swirled in her - her misconceptions and misinterpretations of impulse issued in a nervous excitement or lethargy. She wanted to be alone with the rat man. When the time came for him to leave she would go with him. In the car he looked at her furtively: "I love you - I can't sleep for thinking of you". Here it all was, true to the expected form. He knew what to say, how to look. Part of her thought how stupid he was; another part was thrilled. To have power over a man, to dominate and tantalise him, this was a new pleasure. She didn't reply. The car was at traffic lights. She opened the handle, ran home. The game had begun. It would pass the time. And she liked her new power.

The slim man was thoughtful. He knew something wasn't right, in the relation. But his Persian culture moved him on in negation. He should serve the woman, care for her as a beautiful object. What she wanted should be his wish also. He knew often that what she wanted was nonsense. But still it should be given her. A fierce anger blew up in him. He would allow her what she wanted. But when she came back he would hit her.

The need was to go deeper than either of them could, to look at their own desires. But they were alienated from themselves. Her rich upbringing, in which she had been given all she wanted, had encouraged her to believe that so long as she looked beautiful, all would be granted her. She worked at her appearance, wore expensive clothes. She was mistress of the external form. But meanwhile, inside she was falling apart - her emotions were to be social appearance only, the rest didn't count. And the discarded emotions stayed, locked up inside her, hardly looked at. Only she grew weary, depressed.

It didn't occur to her to wonder why she was like this. She accepted her nervous fits, her morbid absorption in her own health, as the inevitable facts of being female. She couldn't realise how far she had lost herself. And now she wanted to be consoled, to be told by the man that he loved her. She had small sense of her own worth - anything that vindicated her was welcome.

The man she lived with knew she was off track in her own idea of herself. But all the time he felt obliged to serve her in all her whims and desires. Now he had to put himself aside for her to enjoy herself in this new affair. Yet she was also quite dependent on him being there, doing things for her, providing a security. Everything was locked up in falsity.

He heard her coming up the stairs. She wanted to goad the man, strike at him. "Reza, he tells me nice things - he cares for me," she said, jeering as he came in. It was as if she wanted to arouse him, provoke the conflict. Then she would have more power over him because she had put him in the wrong, made him attack her, a woman. In a flash his arms were round her neck and her back pressed against his chest. But he was in control - he wouldn't really hurt her. They were both in a temper, hating each other. He pushed her down, forward, onto the carpet, hitting her as she fell. "You think I love you - well, I hate you. You're nothing to me - you're the kind of man every woman hates". She spoke with fierce stabs of venom. She wanted to undercut him, do him harm. He went out of the room, locked himself in his study. She sat quietly, contemplating the disarray with pleasure. She liked the drama she had made. Both men wanted her. She would be occupied. But there was a deep dissatisfaction: in spite of the drama nothing was real. It wasn't what she wanted.

Reza came round more and more frequently until he was virtually living there. He paid for nothing, ate a lot.

She was rich, let her pay. Occasionally he would state that he intended to pay later. The girl was fascinated by him. She thought he was there just for her, out of desire. She told her friends: "I hate him, he uses us. I want him to go". In fact it would have been easy to be rid of him, had she really wanted this. But she liked him being there. She watched the torture this inflicted on Sayd, the other man. "Why don't you just throw him out?" she asked him, jeeringly. And with part of herself she would have liked this. She was all in pieces with no coherent connection between them. She couldn't connect her fascination with her need for security; her failure to cut off from Sayd took place quite separately in her from her fascinations with Reza. She wanted security with Sayd, fascination with the other. She eyed his neatly pressed blue shirt, folded back with such care, open across his conceited chest, with desire. She also liked it that he cheated them. This showed he was clever. And in Iran to be able to cheat successfully was a good way to be powerful, rich. In some way she equated his deceits with sexual and social power.

How to strike up a real relation? She didn't believe it was possible. There was an ultimate defeat in her. She felt that whatever she tried to do, she was beaten from the start. So what was the point in trying? All that remained were escapes, brief excitements and thrills and the self-hatred, issuing in jeering and torture. She hated herself as a basic premise.

Sometimes she would drive out with Reza to his room at the university. There he would tell her again: "I love you. When I don't see you I can't eat or sleep". There was no physical contact between them. It all went on at the level of stimulation and control. She wanted to keep her power. Meanwhile Sayd was left back at the flat, brooding, seething up his anger. There were regular occasional beatings.

Nothing happened. The emotions followed their twisted course, constantly impure and undifferentiated. It was hard to separate out the real impulse from the false. But they made no effort. At the bottom all three were defeated before they began. They had no belief that it was possible to clarify or create.

Back in Iran the events ran on with no-one in control. It was all disorder. The mullahs were in charge: everyone was blamed by the Iranians except the Iranians themselves. It was America who made the mess, external powers. And America had indeed made much of the mess. But the Iranians had endorsed this so long as it suited them. This they forget. Always they saw themselves blameless. Now, in sentimental gushes, the Shah was praised up again by many. He had been a good man, trying to improve Iran. His secret police, torture camps, imperial fantasies were forgotten. What if he had had these? The idea hung over the majority. "He had been a good man". It was all unthought out. The rich Iranian families sat intact in their rich homes, hoping for a return to the material excesses of the Shah's time. And the weird, disordered emotions ran on everywhere, unreflected on. It was as if the culture itself was collapsing and the power of thought had vanished. Instead a non-belief had arisen. "Nothing can be made clear. Why bother?" Things were as they were. Meanwhile you enjoyed yourself as best you could.

But the unwanted echo crept in, that things were not so enjoyable. In England the girl Maryam was bored in spite of her circumstances - there wasn't enough thrill for her in the situation. Even if she went to Reza's room, undressed, posed and let him photograph her, it didn't dispel her basic misery. She was thwarted. Unable to move forward along any living strand of development she was thrown back only on sensation.

In her imagination she pictured scenes of violent passion; in her body she was still a virgin, almost untouched. Now she let herself be touched, but never sacrificing her virginity. She liked to pose, tantalise. Her fantasy led her also to believe she should have a job, perhaps as a beautician, for which she had some training. In reality she lay on her bed for most of the day taking sedative drugs. She told her friends she wanted an intelligent man to marry, while she let herself stay unevolved, never troubling really to think.

She was brought up to believe that if she dressed well she would be married to a rich man. Then she need do nothing. He would serve her, look after her material needs, do as she ordered. But this upbringing did not fit even with her own confused emotions and thoughts. She was all divided. She had ideas of what she wanted. But between the idea and the achievement were thick barriers. She had no will, no concept of sustained effort. For had not everything been bought for her before? It was easy to buy - you went into a shop, you paid, and you had the object, all with no effort. She didn't even have to earn the money herself. And she had been encouraged to believe that everything was like this. So now she lay inert, wondering why it was all so boring, why she felt always ill.

Her parents were coming to visit her. They wanted her to go back with them, to live in Germany. There the father had his carpet business. He had stayed there, on and off, with his wife for fourteen years. Yet he spoke hardly any German, his wife none. They had kept themselves insulated from European corruption, they believed. Now the father wanted his daughter to follow the predicted path, to marry a rich Iranian man. The husband would take her back to the small German town, or to Teheran, install her in his house. Her other sisters were all married. She should follow the set pattern.

Vaguely she resisted her father. When he phoned she said she wanted to stay in England. Here was a definite impulse. She didn't want to be married off, to settle into the rich life of a married Persian girl. But this was the life she had been prepared for. Her whole upbringing led her to this position. When she was with her father he told her what to wear; he liked smart, rich dresses, elegant hair styles, gold and diamonds. The girl was familiar with his mode - she could carry it off. But somewhere in her was a vague rather weak resistance.

She didn't want to face her own blankness, to realise that she had just been prepared for a rich marriage. She wanted the image for herself of one who could act in her own right. But nothing equipped her for this. She leaned heavily on Sayd for all her practical arrangements. And for thrills there was Reza. What did she do for herself? Her parents sent her money. Now they threatened to cut her off if she didn't do what they wanted. She had to start to act for herself, or else give in.

She was in an undercurrent of desperation. On the surface all went on as before. She flirted with Reza, let him caress her, fell back on Sayd. She was trying to detach herself. Some days she didn't see Reza. But it was too much for her. She could achieve no momentum. Now her parents were almost on her.

She wanted resources to help her against them. Only she felt she belonged to them and could never defy their wishes. To go against them would be to cut herself in pieces yet again. She was a mass of divisions and contradictions.

She was critical of Sayd. She sensed that he wanted to be fair and just, to do what was right. Partly she admired him for this. Also she found it boring. The other man, who made no pretence of morality was exciting to her, wicked. He was purely selfish, always seeking his own ends, more money for himself, more sex. He had an insect-like mindless pursuit of his own ends, without another consideration. The girl was used to the idea of furtive pleasures; anything that had the air of prohibition drew her to it. But in spite of herself, she was always a spectator. She was never drawn in, finally, into the sin. She could not be the complete bug, encased in its impervious shell, creeping only after its own ends. She liked to watch herself. "So this is me, undressing for this man. So that's him, touching me there". She was her own show. The man Sayd, he was too virtuous. He gave in to her. At first she liked it. But then she wanted other victories. He was too easily defeated. Again came the division. She wanted him to do as she wished. But she was bored, after a while, when he did.

With Reza she used her sensual beauty to tease him; she would talk about sex with him, even strike poses she knew would attract him. There was no full action - she wouldn't lose her virginity. And so she held the man in her power. He, in his turn, could have refused the game, not responded. But there was the chance she might give in. She lost sight of the distorted emotions she aroused in him by her behaviour. A kind of hatred mixed with lust rose up in him. He wanted to kill her for humiliating him, keeping him off her. On the surface he was fair and urbane. This seemed almost a norm, for Persian men and women. They would lock each other in a mixture of hate and lust, and revel in the drama that unfolded. On the surface came the statements of love and desire, from the man. They were a sham, a cover for lust and an urge to destroy, shatter the woman. The man's sperm would act as an implant of venom in the female body, sending out waves of friction into her veins, the impulse to destroy in her turn. The women realised the statements were part of the game, but acted as if they believed them. She would not give her sexuality up to the poison. She wanted homage, attention, flattery, in exchange for whatever she gave.

The parents sat in the square room. The father was old, with a distinguished air - he walked with a stick, his broad shoulders bent. There was a latent, cruel dominance, behind the caring front. The mother was well-dressed and silent. She had been married since she was 15. She had no opinions, or so it seemed, never beginning any conversation, just joining in rather timidly once one had started. Their daughter sat on the floor opposite them. She looked younger and more relaxed with them there. Reza had gone off, keeping out of the way. He knew her parents wouldn't like him. She had almost forgotten him. He was just a distraction, a device she used to amuse herself. Sayd was still there, talking to the father politely and respectfully. She liked to abuse him and let her parents hear, hint to them that she despised him.

The parents talked of opening a shop for her in England. It was a front. Their real purpose was to take her back with them. The other offer was to present the guise of reasonableness. But it was easy enough to find reasons why a shop was impossible. There was no work permit available, for example. So they were set on taking the daughter back.

"You should be ashamed," the mother told the daughter on a shopping trip. "You could have a nice flat, all you wanted. Instead you stay here. You should have children". The daughter knew what was expected of her. She should marry a rich Persian man, be kept by him. Perhaps she would do this. She could feel all the reserves of resignation in her that would allow such a course. And it would all be sanctioned as doing what her parents wanted. What else was there in life anyway? To sit in a rich room, to give orders, be pandered to: this could be her life. Only it seemed like a defeat. However, the fact that she had been brought up for this meant perhaps it was foolish to struggle.

She began to drift, let another's will take over hers. After her moods of self-insistence had subsided, there came new moods of resignation and submission. So she alternated in phases between irritable domineering and virtual passivity or indifference. For she knew she was only a woman and ultimately useless, even suspect. What good was it, to resist? Her parents knew her character. She would rebel, protest for a while, then return back to the mould they chose for her. Then, that mould completed, she would revert to moods of domination and commands inside it. Such moods were the sign that she didn't really believe she could change her circumstances but neither did she like them. They were the convulsions of a strangled self that nonetheless she believed could never by anything other than strangled. And like many Persian women she was moody, whimsical, because this was one way to assert herself. But the assertion was always within a cage.

The cage itself was lavish, plush. One of the main conditions of the restriction was wealth and richness. The chairs in the prison were of the finest quality. The wives there wore the most splendid clothes and jewels. She could be a fine figure, so long as she confined herself to the appropriate behaviour and endorsements. She could sulk, be irritable, if she chose. The man would accept this. Was it not a sign that the woman was purely feminine, that she made such weird displays? She could command him for gifts and services. He would enjoy providing these. They were a reflection of his power in the outer world, and also of his power over the woman. He had the power to confer such things, expensive goods, activities, while she had none. All she could confer were moods of tractability or gentleness if she chose, or her sexuality, or her appearance. So her exercise of power was largely in her moods. The women came to expect lavish gifts from their men; hardly any of them viewed these as a kind of domination. Yet few of them were happy either. There was a nervous restless friability about them, in spite of all the assertion. Should the girl become like these?

She had no conscious idea of her reluctance. She wasn't capable or trained to make thoughtful interpretations of her own feelings. No alternative imaginative vision drew her on. She rather thought that she would submit. She imagined herself as the elegant hostess, in the latest fashion, with rich jewellery: she quite liked the image. All would admire her. The man was almost irrelevant - so long as he was reasonably good in appearance, that was enough. For it was mainly in externals that such a marriage existed, in making a good show.

Her parents watched the television. They moved unquestioningly in the world. The mother liked most of all to go shopping - she could buy all she wanted. This was her main form of self-expression. To identify the preferred object, take the money from the purse, feel the bag with the goods inside in her hand - these were her greatest joys. In the daytime the mother and daughter would tour the shops, just spending money.

She could not think, it was beyond her. The conditions of her life were what she should submit to, that was all. Only her morbid interest in diseases increased. She would speculate about her own health, over and over. She didn't see Reza for several days. It seemed he could pass easily in and out of her life. He was a sensation, momentary. The reality was this fixity with Sayd. But she didn't want to submit to it. She must always attack him, try to strike him down.

The waves of death came flowing up, out of some centre in her, darkening her consciousness, her very sight. Things looked darker to her, in this depression. Could she only devolve? There seemed to exist only disbelief or fatality in her. Nothing stirred to any living purpose.

Her parents would soon go back to Germany. She would stay here. She was fixed on this. She would stay with Sayd, partly hating him, but dependant. She cast around for other people to suck into her vacancy. She could be kind, generous with friends. But mainly she lived like a ghost, unable to enact or move. She liked to sit in her hot square room, in a daze, in front of the electric fire that was always on, lazy and indulgent. She could stir for nothing.

What man would take her like this? Plenty of Persian men would desire her for her looks. But who would take her beyond the preset norms? She would stay fixed down in the mould.

She pulled her fur coat closer around her. She didn't feel well, she would go shopping. Nothing was resolved.

Quite late one night, the doorbell rang. The old father was already asleep. The mother was moving gently about the room, putting clothes away. The girl went down the stairs to the front door. It was Reza. She had almost forgotten him. He didn't matter to her now. "What are you here for?" she asked him sharply. "I have nowhere to say - I thought I would go to where my friends were". He knew by introducing the word 'friends' he could exploit the Persian habit and duty of hospitality. He was obliged to be fed and housed.

She felt her heart sink. She was to be abused even now. She knew he didn't love her, that it had all been a game for him too. She hated him, for this. A sort of incoherence overwhelmed her. Her parents were upstairs; now this new pressure had come to oppress her. She felt her own resources draining out. She wanted to collapse into herself, become void.

The next day the tensions twisted and turned in her. She was strange, unusual to herself. The kitchen objects had a curious hallucinatory touch to them. She couldn't think or reflect. Reza was there, in Sayd's room, her parents also. She felt she was suffocating, gripped by a weird sickness. Here was one solution, to lapse into illness. Then she would not have to face the reality. Also she really was ill. Her parents found her in the kitchen trembling and vomiting. She spoke in a sham incoherence. She knew she wasn't really so ill. But she wanted to lapse into passivity.

They took her to the casualty department. The Persians used this part of the hospital as a General Practitioner's. She just needed a tranquillizer, the doctor said. She was led home again. Reza had gone.

How could she break the cycle, get onto some new strand? She would go shopping again. Inside herself she felt doomed to be ineffectual. What could she do? She would wait for a while to see what happened. There was a kind of endurance needed. She wouldn't go back with her parents. Maybe later, when all else had failed.

She realised she was nervous, neurotic, on her own, in spite of Sayd's attentions. She could only be herself in anxiety. She hoped, vaguely, for some deep revelation or unmistakable emotion to fall on her like a vice from some external position. Then her life would be settled.

The shops distracted her, she was in abeyance, unreal.

MAGREB

He stood waiting in the dust at the side of the road. That morning, like so many, he had walked up the whitened path from the house, to wait for the ride to work. Behind the cracking wall of the small stadium opposite he saw the tower of the mosque lit up with plastic lights in the dawn, like a garish ornament. The taxi slowed down, stopped.

There was a queer tang to the morning, as if something long expected was at last to happen. The driver turned to him, looking ill and thin, muttering in Arabic, about the radio. He didn't understand. The car passed the small, broken shops with the men already outside the cafés, the butchers with cows' heads stuck on poles outside. It was all hopeless and forlorn, everyone ragged. The road crossed a railway, then ran past an inland lake towards the airport, with a wood on one side. Rubbish had been tipped on each side of the road and scattered beneath the trees. Thin dogs wandered there. An early flight was arriving, perhaps from Europe, losing height over the dirty lake. He watched the plane drop almost to the tree tops, sway, then vanish out of sight onto the runway beyond the trees. He wanted to be away himself.

So often he had made this trip. The car sped on, past the barracks that bordered the airport. The soldiers were kept ready, to go to kill the people if there was "unrest". Serious unrest was unusual, the people being in general so passive. But last year, after bread prices had been doubled, people had run up the main street smashing windows. In suburbs post offices had been burned, cars hijacked. The army had opened fire, killing sixty rioters. The threat was always present, to make the reprisal.

Outside the barracks waited police on fast motor bikes and a line of grey buses with meshes over the windows. These could travel fast to any part of the city which threatened disturbance.

He was uneasy, as always. Nothing seemed to happen, on any extensive scale, but each day an "incident" would occur. Some protestors would be arrested, men from rival political groups would fight, someone might be thrown out of a window, chained up, his legs broken. There was an under feeling of spite and frustration. Any European in the street would have to tolerate the cumulative spite and silent resentment of those he passed. In the car he knew it was partly legitimate. The people had no reason to love Europe. They wanted their own identity as an Arabic world. At the same time they wanted the Western things, technologies, facilities. So it was a contradiction. They were always poorer, ridiculous, to the Europeans. So their reasoning ran. They wanted to be an Arab state, rich and powerful, dealing revenge. Instead they were impotent, jeered at. A hard anger rose in them, at this condition. The land was volatile, waiting to rise up.

The road ran now as a broad highway, like a motorway, only without being finished off - the tarmac spread brokenly into the dusty gutters, and a man herded goats along an unfenced edge. The cars ran very fast. On each side blocks of concrete flats rose out of a scrubby grassland. They were running round the southern limit of the city. The Hilton Hotel stood up unrelated to the land, the centre where rich businessman stayed.

After some miles the urban landscape diminished. On each side of the road were fields with a few horses ploughing, and then more barracks, then a small town again, with the city lunatic asylum. Men walked in the streets, unshaven, in pyjamas, sheep and goats ran in front of cars. A cow's head stared down from a pole, a lunatic addressed the passing cars, while dusty men looked on.

Why was the foreigner here? Each day he came from the house to the university, taking the same route. The land had no need of him. He knew its Arab Nationalist aims, could agree with those, knowing also how little his own endorsement or not was required. At the road junction to the university the army officer waved the car through, the grey emergency buses lined up close by. Inside men sat edgily with their guns pointing upwards, the butts on the floor, the barrels level with the meshed window.

Each day was the same. Nothing happened, only all was ominous with some expectation. He heard the clatter of the army helicopters overhead as they neared the campus. The roofs of the university buildings loomed up spartan behind high walls, bizarre in the open countryside. Sited so far from the city, it had been reasoned, the students could do little harm in the city itself. They couldn't go and smash anything, unless they tore the plants themselves up out of the fields.

He saw the group like a black swarm by the main gate. The army men stood near, watching. Great cries in Arabic were going up. The crowd was marching, as usual, in the campus yard, shouting as it went. Between low buildings, cheaply erected and flimsy, stretched grass and a wide paved pathway. The slogans, shouted out, painted on the wall, stuck on sheets, meant nothing literally to the man. But the meanings you could intuit. The group, as it marched in the dust round the campus yard, struck him as sinister and justified. A wave of hate, against the West, against the regime of the Arab land, was being sent out. The guards at the gate returned the hate. The soldiers in the buses sat on restlessly.

At the end of the compound posters hung on the wall in neat Arabic script. The shouting died away as he moved into the staff place. No-one else had arrived yet. He looked round the room, which had never ceased to strike him as alien. What was he doing here? The place wasn't his. He had no centre in that land. The land belonged to the people outside.

Perhaps the other teachers wouldn't come. They might simply stay at home. Or else the army would refuse them access to the entry road. Anything could happen. He hardly cared. The outer disruption of the society, the division into rival sections of mutual hatred, had its parallel in his own mind. He was zoned up, into fragments at war. Like a piece of rotating machinery, he turned from fragment to fragment, cyclical. All was incoherent and struggling. Why was it all in pieces? A heavy disillusion pulled him down.

He watched the shadow of the helicopter hovering above the yard, saw the dust swirl, was delivered from his reflexions by the beat of the rotor. The soldiers were throwing small concrete blocks down onto the students. A few struck them. The helicopter banked away. He watched the perspex door sliding shut, the black leather arm of the pilot's assistant pull back in, as the craft moved on. The students were excited, tending the two or three who had been injured.

He went out into the hall, to see what he could do. A dense crowd of agitators was pressed right up to the glass doors of the building and the whole courtyard was full. Slowly he realised it had become impossible to leave. A Tunisian teacher approached him from the secretary's office.

"You see, it's as we expected." He looked at the foreign man, quizzically.

"Yes, and it's needed. There have got to be protests."

"It will achieve nothing."

The Tunisian was negative, defeated. He had been part of the same situation so often before. The ruling powers absorbed the demonstrations like a sponge: nothing, in fact, was lastingly achieved by them. And yet, better they should take place, than not.

The foreign teachers could not join in. The students would permit no-one but those of their race to participate. So the foreigners were pushed out onto a limb, speculating. The English man felt futile, under these conditions. He should leave the country, leave it to its own inhabitants to settle its fate. He would have liked to assist in the revolution, only here it would not be possible.

A great cry went up outside, and the crowd surged back suddenly, smashing the doors by accident. A few students ran into the hall-way. In the distance, up by the gates, like a societal hallucination, he saw the truncheons raised, the

cloud of tear gas drifting. The army had got tired of waiting and had made a rush into the courtyard. A few shots
were fired, casually, like afterthoughts. The rattle of the
helicopters overhead blurred the gunfire.

These were men fighting in the last fifteen years of the
twentieth century, for what? A dictator in power, allied to
the West, a system of administration that doesn't work,
wide-spread poverty and unemployment, a layer of wealth
out of most people's reach: the status quo protects itself.
On the other side, those who suffer. The friction of the one
part grating on the other, on and on, with the prevailing
powers so far dominant. It was all like the inner psyche,
divided against itself, in attrition.

The clouds of gas drifted past the windows, abstract.
The students were running. The soldiers stood at the gates,
the guns hanging down. About two or three figures lay
immobile in the yard. In the dust spots of blood formed,
red on white. The figures were left where they were. The
students had retreated into a faculty building opposite the
gate, at the far end of the campus. There was silence. A
moderate wind blew the gas into the fields. The bodies lay
on, inert, in the yard.

The sun lit up the wall opposite the window of the
teachers room. All seemed unreal. The two men sat in
silence.

"It's as usual, two killed." The Tunisian was the first to
speak. He was agitated, upset. "And now, they will perhaps go away." A helicopter clattered nearer, hovering to
pick up the immobile figures. Dust blew over the blood on
the ground, stuck to the wounds. The campus was quiet
now, with no shouting, uncanny.

Was this all the latest incident amounted to? The ominous silence hung on over the simple buildings. The hatred
had been expressed, squirted out in a small climax. The
sun shone down into the yard, making the dust burn. The
university was frugal, not at all luxurious, more like a
barracks. The place had no meaning, so remote and incon-

gruous in the countryside, except as a focus of dissent.

"Shall we go?" The Tunisian was cool. Such events were normal. He wanted to get home to his wife.

"How?"

"We'll just drive out."

Outside there was no movement. In the distance, out in the fields, you could hear the voice of a student agitator hectoring his fellow-students. The main gate was deserted, save for a single vehicle. A hot wind blew from the desert. At the gate the guards saluted. No reference was made to the disturbance. Officially the army was there to protect the staff from the students. The grey vans of the riot control unit had moved off down the lane, stopping just out of sight round a slight bend. Only the grey roofs were visible through the leaves of a hedge. The guards were assuming the two teachers would be on the President's side. The bodies in the yard were no longer visible, transported away by the helicopter.

Gradually the city enclosed them once more as they drove. He looked out of the windows at the cracked buildings, set out in ugly lines on each side of the road. The place was amorphous, just a conglomerate of parts, zones of poverty. A great tiredness now filled him, as if he could hardly breathe. There was a knot of tension and disbelief. Was this the world? It seemed so.

The car passed further in, towards the centre. The traffic was all around. There was no relief. There were the two bodies, lying inert, first in the dust, now in some military installation, out of sight. They were harbingers of what was to come. The bigger blows remained, to be dealt later.

The Deviant

She was creeping along, the poison at work. Below her plausible self, of seeming rational debate, she was fixed, as if in evil. A dangerous, helpless mode emerged in her bent movement, the neck craning, bending in weakness and cunning. For the neck could straighten, the tongue whip out and cut. Then the bent submissive stance would be resumed.

She was middle aged, one of the dangerous ones. Through weakness she had made every aspect of her life a failure, and now in ashiness she counted the cost. Her will, though, she held intact, malevolent above the wreckage. She must have her way now, her ideas must triumph, die what else might. Everyone else was there to be overridden by her. She was lonely, so in egotism she would use any-one - everyone - to fill her own vacancy up. Sentimental terms were one side of the weak mind; 'lonely', 'sharing' were the evil watch words. If you let her share with you, up it would come, the weakness, the abuse, the vanity, the suffering fantasies. Yes, yes, she had always been good, meant so well, and the world had been hard, harder to her than anyone. At the same time she clung fiercely, like a hard bug on a wall, to her job, earning in the wage. She was wealthy, having inherited capital, shares, from her factory owning father, almost enough to live freely on. But she liked to ape poverty, finding this convenient for her mask of the liberal. It wasn't she who was on the side of the capitalist. Yet all the time the shares were being han-dled for her by a stockbroking brother, mounting up the cash. Some were even investments in weapons companies. But, in avant-garde carelessness she protested she didn't know what her investments were; her brother had carte blanche. He was a high Conservative, working for the party at local level.

She was lying ill in bed. Her husband was downstairs in the luxury Swiss home. She had come here, straight from her parents' home, to be paid for in upper class marriage to the Swiss businessman. How hard done to she felt! She lay in revenge between the sheets, her mad brain turning

71

over this and that. She would like to bring on a cancer, flaunt the bulging growth, to punish them all. Downstairs sat her three daughters, breathing in the nervous negation she pumped out, instruments to provide the sympathy she craved. They were hers, to do as she liked with, The small girls heard her croak out, "Elfride! Elfride!" She was calling the youngest.

The girl climbed miserably up the stairway. Already, at eight, she was used to depression, queer fits of abuse in the family. A flatness was in her eyes, she would give random starts of fear. In a dream she saw snakes crawling in the house, blue, red, garish. She jerked open the door of the sickroom. The thin hand projected from the sheet, bony and grasping.

"My darling, darling, hold my hand tighty-tight". The wasted fingers of the neurotic grasped the clean white hands of the small girl. With the touch a wave of poison crossed the skin, entered the child's being. The seeds of further weakness crossed in the air, through also the skin membrane and cells.

"I'm ill, my little lovely. Daddy doesn't love me. He loves money, money, money. But you love me". The child wanted to recoil, fling herself out of the room. Only a dim child's instinct to help, to make it all right, kept her there listening to the wild crooned words. Did it all rest on her, to make the family well? An awful impotence seized her, turning the blood anxious. All was insecure, rocking about her. The woman's voice ran on, at a higher note. It had a resonant, hypnotising timbre that echoed in the room, like a sinister medium repeating in hysteria the pseudo words of a supposed spirit. "You see Daddy's given mummy cancer, I may have cancer. You remember your cousin died of cancer of the brain last year. Well, like her I may be. When they operated they found a lot of pus in her growth . . ."

The child watched and listened as the harm ran out. The mother liked anecdotes of medical disaster, to hear of illnesses. She built up narratives around them. Then the child saw her mother dead, and with twenty knives multi-coloured in her naked, thin body, with the serpenty bent neck. Her mother was the snake who slid noiseless in the house, with the venom in her, the poison of uselessness. She should run or stamp on the creature's neck but she was paralysed, transfixed. The mother squeezed her hand. "Run out, and play. Don't worry about me." The daughter trailed miserably away, the burden set in her blood, the heavy stricture of the other's neurosis eating her own nervous power away.

The father was out, more and more, on business. A simple man, he could not grasp the bitter incapacity his wife involved him in. She had seemed plausible, in England, the upper-middle class daughter - unattractive, but due for an inheritance. The ugliness was offset by advantages he hoped to gain from her social class. Now the doctors had told him she was only mentally unwell. He had offered to pay for her to study, to counteract her crazy claims she had been deprived of this. Her uselessness led her to refuse. Now, below, he heard her bent tread on the stair, the muttering: "My husband earns money. My husband earns money." Down she came, trailing her socks off her feet, her ugly track suit trousers bagging up behind and dirty ragged pullover, inappropriately pink, revolting him.

She wanted to cause trouble, get the girls against him. She kept up the muttering, goading. He watched, hypnotised in his turn, unable to understand. "You earn", she paused "money". She spat in his direction. She was glad to have it, had always been pleased to be so plushly ballasted; her parents too had indulged her. He felt the blood pump quicker in his veins. His hand was out, he would smack her down, obliterate her vileness, the sick female object that muttered. She was a travesty of a female; her skinny, stooping frame and jerking viper's neck disgusted him. The hand knocked her against the banister. She exaggerated her fall, shrieking, drawing the children to her with

73

her cries. "Don't be frightened, my darlings. Don't let him touch you". She lay back, histrionic, small dots of blood on her teeth, on the dirty pink pullover. Yet it was her the children were afraid of. Only she drew them to her, used them as devices in the contest with her husband. She liked to feel herself humiliated, knocked down. Thus she could claim sympathy. She would take revenge on life through the children. She wanted them to suffer as she did, to be as useless as herself. Scared, the small girls looked down at her, made responsible for the adult. They heard their father's car start up. He was gone. "It's so much nicer, just us, my lovelies. See how peaceful it is." The woman crooned, her hypnotic, drugged voice booming. The fact that she had caused the trouble, set it up, was lost to her evasive consciousness. "It's Daddy's fault I might have cancer", she confided. She liked to confide such snippets to her children. It drew her closer to them as she wheedled out sympathy. Secretly she exulted in her own manipulation. Only she mattered. Only she was real. This was her sick credo.

The daughter was choking in her room, in the small flat that looked out onto the main road that crossed the suburb. Elfride's mother had decided to leave the businessman husband. What did it matter if she broke everything up? In the older woman was the lust to smash and tear, at herself and those nearest her. Somewhere in the past, in the English town in the Midlands, the small daughter of the manufacturer had sipped in poison. She was the awkward one, prone to nervous depressed fits, aggressions. All had been done for her, but still she was deviant. She cut up the curtains in her bedroom, was expelled from her school. She worshipped her own sickness like a chef priding himself on a speciality he had invented. Now her own difference would be expressed in leaving. Her husband was glad to be rid of her. He had long since stopped going home, travelling willingly abroad to represent his company. But the youngest daughter, Elfride, now fifteen, was taken with the mother, annexed with her as support and confederate, hypnotised into the mad maternal meanings. This mother saw life lurid; no-one was good enough to know, no task worthy enough for herself or family to attempt.

The girl sat blank in the class, unable to follow. Her head was dead with the monologues of her mother, the acrid undertow of the rows between man and wife. Ever since she could remember the older woman had been an imperious invalid. Suddenly a snake was coiling at the desk leg, another writhing on the gulley for pencils. She bit down the fear, stared ahead, sweating. She had no friends. Her energy was reserved for the thin, stooped figure of the parasite. Somehow the individual circuit of nervous energy in the child had been tapped into the mother's, so the older woman could drink the resources of the younger. Now, alone at home with the older woman, unable to go to school, she would choke in the privacy of her room, her throat heaving and convulsed. Monologues destroyed her power to speak; nothing she said to her mother was reacted to as real, interchange was non existent. Only the droning hard-done-to speeches existed, to be listened to, hypnotising, monotonous.

The older daughter, Martha, almost a simpleton in mind, had fled away months before to live on a Greek beach. Now she was back, walking the streets of the Swiss city, with her boyfriend. She walked on the pavement in the sun, her unpleasant pasty face set on the top of a bony neck and frame. This was another version of the mother, intact and impenetrable. A bent figure suddenly stopped a small car in a traffic stream, bouncing it up the kerb, twisted out of the car door, bent in a shambling, crampy run after the girl. "Martha, Martha, it's your mummy, I love you, wait". Groups of pedestrians watched amused as the bent, crippled-looking figure plunged in indecent run, ugly, after the young people. Her hair was cropped short on her skull, the grey track suit trousers she always wore hung like grotesque nappies over her non-existent buttocks. A shoe lace, undone, flapped in the dust as she ran. Laughing, the daughter and friends climbed in a van and drove off, leaving the bent figure in the road, panting, hand on hip, shouting "My lovely! I love you! Come back!"

Back in the flat the youngest daughter was burning her books. One by one she slashed them up first with a razor blade. She had been good at school, could go on to university if she persisted. Now it was over. Language, attention, sense were destroyed. The snakes danced, writhing in heaps about the room. Her eye-lids had puffed up, ugly, in the stress not to see. Over her flesh queer red blotches had formed, as if the skin itself was trying to grow an extra protection. The door slid open and the jerking head of her mother was suddenly there, blind and silent to anything but her own narrow concerns. She didn't notice the ruined books, Elfride's condition. Her attention was fixed only on herself, "I'm so glad you're here. I've got awful problems." She turned as she spoke to Elfride, putting on her pity-me look, then sat bent at the table, head in hands. The daughter wanted to crush her as she sat, kick her to the ground. Instead she watched, in guilt. "Help me! Help me! I can't help it!" The mother began to scream and scream. "I can't help it! I can't help it!" Objects fell to the ground as she scrabbled on the table top, and flecks of foam whitened the thin lips of the bitter, elder wife. "Bugger the world!" She began to throw herself about, whimpering in her own ugliness. With a shambling, twisty jerk she took herself off to her room, lay face-down on the bed, weakly.

Although used to such scenes - they had been part of her life for as long as she could recall - Elfride was each time aghast again, ashamed. She was dependent on this woman as her mother. From her should come shelter, food, care. Instead all was inverted. She, Elfride, was expected to provide support, buy and cook the food, clean the flat, listen to the monologues and outbursts. It was thus that her capacity to study had vanished, sucked away by the pump of the mad woman's demands. Yet outside the house the mother kept herself plausible, upper middle class, eccentric but liberal. Inside she indulged herself, let herself go, used anyone up who came her way.

The daughter could not cut loose. Somehow she had been made to feel responsible. A clear bright light like in a surgical theatre shone cold through the window, from the Alps. This was her life, then; this was all. The room was clearly lit in its banality, the dirty carpet scattered with plastic bags full of her mothers teaching books, dirty pairs of her pants lying loose on the ground. She could hear the grunts and jerks of the woman behind the door, imagine the scene in there. The mother would lie face down on her bed, sometimes curling into the foetal position, whine out, "I want to run away" over and over again, call in her daughter and clutch her hands bonily in hers. Outside, though, she was able to be the respected teacher, the drawling high class English woman with enlightened and sensitive views, insights into psychology. How hard it had been to break away from her philistine husband! How ill he had made her! So she put it about, about herself, coaxing sympathy out of anyone she met. Meanwhile, at home, she terrorised her youngest daughter with her fits and domineering. She was Lena, entitled to all. Had not her children come out of her womb? They were hers and she would eat them. Her rejection by Martha made her keen to tighten her grip on Elfride.

There was to be no more school. Elfride went instead to the psychiatrist. She sat in the room, the younger girl, ugly in her own depression, the skin blotchy with rashes and marks. She was silent and couldn't talk.Then she lay on the bed in the tiny flat alone, the medicaments in pots around her; sometime she took too many, had to be taken to hospital by friends who'd called in, to have them pumped out. The mother began now to thrive, outwardly. She was conveniently indifferent to her daughter's suffering. She put the pain down to a 'phase' or 'life', hardly thinking of it or connecting it with herself. She returned to Elfride only late at night. The girl depressed her, broke her triumph at being a divorced woman. Sometimes the mother hung her head round the door, the red mouth contorted, twisted up in abuse: "You're the reason Daddy left us." The mother had come to believe this. "You were a naughty bugger, a bugger". The slaps began to fall. The girl backed away as the serpent shape advanced, the crimson lipstick on the old clenched lips gleaming lurid. The bony hand descended, she saw the knuckles white, the wedding ring. The mother was out of control, hitting out, smashing down the book shelves. The girl skipped aside, watched.

"You see, my little lovely. I'd do anything for you". Now the mother moved in switched persona to clutch the daughter round the head, pull her to her in would-be affection. She wanted to forget her violence. "In every family there's rows. It's best to let out. Much more honest." In her eyes her abuse sessions now had come to seem like virtues. "Aunty Kay never let out. And look, she got that cancer. It was awful, awful. As big as a baby's head". The daughter watched and listened, powerless. Her mother intoned the narrative, hypnotising, in trance-like tones. "I'd do anything for you". This was her fantasy conviction. Instead of use, abuse, she was the actual benefactor. "You'd have nowhere to go if it wasn't for me, my sweetie one." The room swelled and fell in waves of madness. The girl's mind was unhinging more. Perhaps it was right, to let out. Perhaps she was cared for. Perhaps all families were like this one. Only why did she feel sick, the snakes dance? "Let's watch tel, together, just us two. It's so-o nice together." The mother led her to the settee, sat stroking her hair as the film progressed, working insidiously to take her over. It was her whim and will now that Elfride would submit, would accept the fantasy of maternal care. "That silly school, all those exams, who cares, dearie!" The poison words, sapping effort, motivation, switching all to the nihilism of the older woman's sick view ran like intoxicants into the blood. Now, alone, this woman needed a slave and nurse; to humour her narratives, endorse her fits and mad outbursts. This was the true sharing. She could send the girl also on errands to get and cook food, even to her father's house to reclaim the mother's goods. There was no thought to spare the daughter anything, make her path less hard. The father had changed the locks, forbidden the elder woman to go near. He had a horror of her creeping figure, bending and stooping its way up the drive. The children were contaminated by her, he rightly surmised. There was no point in bothering with them.

Elfride was in the bar, not at home. The older men gathered round. She would go back with them, have the sex. They might look after her, save her from the mad room with her mother. She wanted to be loved. They had their pleasure with the teenager, left her alone. She recalled the thrust of the penis, the splash of white when the men finished, slipped out of her. So she had at least one power, could be wanted for at least one thing. The deadness crept round her in the family, in the men, in her own momentary thrill; nothing mattered. The music beat up, the chrome lamps shone, men would approach her. The snakes whispered to her, confused now with the bent serpent and the white, spongy penises. Who was she to value herself? Let anyone abuse her who liked. That was her merit. She would follow in her mother's footsteps, run in self-hatred against creative impulse, cut herself about. Her mother encouraged her. "Yes, yes, it's right to be erotic. I never was. And look how my marriage turned out." Going with the men was blandly interpreted as 'being erotic'. This was the convenient view. Vicarious, the older woman egged the girl on to further conquests. Nothing mattered.

The plausible self was persistent on the surface of the mother. Time passed and work, teaching, centred more and more in her life. She was welcome at young peoples' gatherings at the college, so open and emancipated. So long as no-one thwarted her she could keep her fits secret.

A little round of seeing her daughters who all lived nearby kept up the fancy that the past was all over. But there would sometimes come up the irritable mood, in which she should hit out; she had fantasies of spraying people with her own piss, men at work she imagined had put her down, anyone who had made her jealous. In secret she exulted that she was best, finest, wisest. She worked hard to get people in her control, see things as queerly as she saw them. All she ever saw was herself, reflected back as she liked. If anyone didn't reflect her back as she liked, the hatred would rise, extreme and acrid. The past was locked up in herself in a not-to-be opened canister. If anyone had been unpleasant it certainly wasn't she. For wasn't she a member of the English upper middle class who always want what's best and act well? If her daughters had run away, lost educations, been destructive and promiscuous, then that was life's affair, none of her doing. If her husband had loathed her, that had nothing to do with herself. A false view of herself split off and floated out to blot her consciousness. Behind this fantasy self lurked the psychic canister, loaded with its self-damning realities. No-one should penetrate there. Was she not the jolly lady, generous and understanding? Her vice now was to fly out at her youngest daughter, keep her under by bullying and spoiling. The elder, Martha, was too similar to herself to be effectively used; she would just go away if offended. So with her it was sickly flattery, back and forth. The joint nervous system ran its interrelated course, still seeping its disorder into Elfride. The younger woman couldn't understand her revulsion when the mother was near. They had all got over it. In fact there had been nothing to get over, so the mother would repeat. Yet sometimes the mother would rub a little excrement onto her cheeks, and quickly wash it off, in secret punishment. Her room, too, she kept filthy, the carpet dusty and strewn with old bills and newspapers. Here she lurked, still in her nappy trousers, ugly, almost epicene, giving out wisdom to anyone who would listen. She knew all about life, so she gave off. She liked evaluating others, often criticising them for making insufficient 'effort'. But still came the moods of violence, smashing up.

Elfride was getting away. Married, she couldn't respond to the influence so totally. The mother was put out. Blood was thicker than water was her favourite axiom. Worse, the daughter was pregnant. "How do you feel, my little love?" The older woman asked with unctuous concern, her voice slimy with false emotion. Underneath the concern, the closeted self was arousing. To break away, no longer be her thing! Against her will, Elfride was drawn back to visit the mother more often. The hypnotised habit, begun so long ago, was reinforced. Cunning, Lena was all concern. "Why don't you stop here, when he's away on business? You don't want to be lonely."

It was a game with the older woman to call any man 'He' in dismissive put-down. She would draw the daughter into intimate collusion if she could. "We can eat together and keep each other company". Elfride pondered. Some queer force was driving her to agree. In the kitchen the mother bared her thin vermilion lips, took up a chicken carcass from the oven, and darted bent to her room to pluck it into her mouth with her hands. Her dirty pullover was stained with drips of grease. Then she returned to the fridge and took two bars of chocolate from a pile of five, and ate them, rapid and shifty. "Watch tel, lovey, have a rest". A tiredness started in the girl and the baby moved restless in the womb, as if troubled by the new, louder voice. She was seven months pregnant.

The man was away, trying to get a job. She came to sleep at her mother's, drawn by a queer compulsion, sometimes lying on a mattress on the floor in the woman's room. "That's right, dearie, we're sharing now". The older woman drew more energy for her school work from the girl's presence, fuelled herself on it. "I like to see the lights on when I come back." She bent from her bed to twist the girl's face to hers, planted a kiss on her cheek with her small, tight mouth, leaving a smudge of red, like blood. The powerlessness was coming back to Elfride.

Each evening, now, for hours, the mother told rambling, incoherent anecdotes about her work, how all there were against her, because she was a woman alone. Then, in the morning, the older woman gave a lift to the exhausted daughter, to work. At night she would want to ferry her home, disguising intent with a genial "Just passing". There was nothing in her life but this coexistence with the girl, her girl. She exulted the man was away, throwing her head back in a raspy laugh when she was alone, pressing her hands onto the sink edge, as she bent over the filthy plates she heaped up there and never washed. How it was all going her way!

The husband was to return. Wearily he descended the road towards the sewage works by the river. In a block next to these the mother lived. The block was old, run down. Here the older woman, Lena, didn't have to 'keep up standards' as she put it. The rent was cheap, so she could hoard up even more cash by living on a high salary where, logically, only the poor should live. Below her hysteria, she was very careful with her own interests. He heard the voices raised, as he climbed the stairs. "You didn't share it with me, you bitch; I'm low-down, I'm not good enough. After all I've done for you. You didn't tell me about your day." As he opened the door he saw the mother was slapping and foaming, hitting out at the pregnant woman. Slivers of food clung to her pullover, since she had overturned her plate, starting up, out of control, and she spat out strands of saliva. She wanted to revile the world, shriek to it that she was vile, and so was it. Her daughter had resisted her, had suddenly refused to tell her where she'd been. The collusion she'd craved had broken. "Ungrateful bugger! After I had you here, to look after you!"

"But you wanted me to come. To keep you company,

you said. No-one said anything about looking after me." Lena ignored the real comment. "Yes, yes, I'm lonely, I'm old." The fit waned, the sentimental, oily tone began. The upper middle class drawl asserted itself, loud, domineering. "Yes, I'll do anything for you". But in the bathroom the red show began and the baby in the womb no longer moved. When the small, perfectly formed corpse was cut out, a clot had passed to block the cord that brought it life. "The blood had stopped. It's nothing to do with me." The older woman was explaining, a few days later. Her eyes narrowed, sensing danger, as she blearily eyed the two parents' faces in front of her. No-one else was real. "And we're so much closer now, sharing the trouble."

The man's arm was fast, swinging down to hit her across the face. She reeled with the blow, and blood flecked on her teeth where her lips were cut. It was as her husband had hit her. Both men had to control themselves, hard, not to exterminate the female creature they loathed. She fell in hysteria on the floor. The daughter eyed her in contempt. "You're a vile bag", she pronounced coolly, "an old parasite child murderer". The mother was moaning, "I love you, dearie, dearie". Cunning, she writhed a little to exaggerate the pain. She wanted to ward off other blows. Buglike, she wanted to preserve herself. But they were tired of her. She wasn't worth their trouble. The doctors had been bewildered about the baby. "The event is so unusual, so rare, with the baby so healthy. But we can't say, definitely, that stress or shock was a factor". So the mother could wriggle free, evade her daughter's verdict, in the inconclusive evidence, save herself in her own sight.

The older woman, Lena, sponged herself in her bath, with the letter showing the rise in her share prices on a table beside her. The long, thin revolting body, with no breasts, just bony ribs jutting, eddied under the surface water. In her a deadness circulated that was constant, There was the job, her daughters, they were all. These she should feed on. Now one was gone. The grandchild was dead. She wondered briefly why it had happened. Already in her own mind she was blameless, exonerated. It was just 'life' that had turned it out like that. Her abuse and attack were forgotten, slipping easily out of her mind. Aunty Kay had that cancer. It had just come on. Her body looked to her like an object, undesirable, nothing. But her will and energy were sharp, in compensation, to her own interests and comforts. She began to pull faces in the mirror, twisting her mouth to ugliness. "I'm ugly, ugly, ugly", she revelled. Then she emerged, dried, lipsticked, dressed, the upper middle class English psyche restored. She was off to a party at her school, where she would tell a modified version of events, putting herself in the best light she could contrive.

The man and woman had gone. She had watched them pass across the bridge over the river, disappear under its wooden, dark medieval roof, raging in cursing powerlessness, to see them leave her. In the mirror her red lips buckled into a bow of acrid song. "I'm fucking glad I killed the child." She tried on the words again. Yes, she was glad. Like that woman who had axed up babies, ten year olds, in her room, then repented and been a Christian. That was it: murder them, find excuses later. She had nothing to give anyone. All should be given her. She opened her wardrobe, looked coldly at the expensive clothes, Armani, Versace, she hoarded up and never wore. She would dress up, be plausible for the school event. She puckered her lips: "Mummy, mummy". She was recalling the old snob who had brought her up and who she still revered as a wonderful English lady. Then a thin laugh rattled in her tight throat as she dressed. She'd be vile and punish the world. She was no-one, so she'd do what she wanted. She couldn't help it.

What he'd done to her, that man, He, the daughter's husband, how unkind, how undeserved! It wasn't true that she'd killed the unborn child. No, she loved little children, darlings, she'd do anything . . . she just wanted love. The slapping, reviling self was gone, tidied away as if it hadn't existed. That woman, with the axes, she'd probably washed the blood off the blades, gone out looking nice, red lipstick. Why shouldn't she? The world was vile, nothing mattered. The refrain ran low in her head, "I'm fucking glad I killed the child." She liked her expensive cosmetics, you needed a little luxury when you get older. You get cancer, if you don't spoil yourself. The lips with white foam formed the words of a song, 'I killed a baby', then she switched on the television, settled in for a coffee before she left. Now she was lonely, furious and they were gone. The phone receiver at her ear and mouth, she dialled the other daughter, spoke loud and jaunty: "Hello, darling, I'm so worried about you, haven't heard". An arrangement was made to meet next day.

The small coffin blazed up in the gas furnace, the funeral a post-medical examination event, clinical and unattended. The baby had been probed. There were no abnormalities. Elfride was blank, dead too, for the moment. Had it really been her mother's fault? Lena was laughing, cackling, rocking in front of the television, her bars of chocolate ranged beside her. Inside herself the black canister containing her reality stayed sealed up tight and safe. She was making herself comfortable again, the privileged English style.

The Reprisal

It was for the money that he'd done it, worked in this way. The signs were all around, as he sat. All the marks were there, of one who had succeeded. The house was large, in the discreet avenue, with other houses set in their own gardens on each side. In the rooms the objects and fittings proclaimed expense, comfort. He was up.

In the adjoining room his wife sat watching television. In the spacious area with its low chairs he felt at home. Together they sat and watched the programmes. It was a crime series; he liked the story and the luxury settings, the action sequences. The man and the woman sat in silence, looking in.

The morning of the meeting broke. He'd relaxed, watching the programmes, and now was alert, ready for the money-making. In the kitchen, he drew down the cereal pack from the luxury kitchen units he'd had installed a month ago. He was always buying, making things 'stylish', as he put it. The suit was the same, expensive material, well-designed. His wife lay asleep as he prepared.

The car backed out of the tarmac driveway. In the kerb he'd had lights set so guests could see their way in for the drinks parties. He'd liked it when they'd complimented him on the improvement. His mind was full merely of money schemes and expenditure. What to buy, where, how to impress. He liked it, that his company was a success, importing items from abroad for customers, exporting; 'big customers' he told himself. There was also the selling of British goods abroad. He was reputed as a middleman in many international deals. Known for his discretion, the government had lately started to use him in deals requiring tact. For example, it was a fact that foreign governments need military equipment, yet might themselves seem questionable, viewed from one angle. So he would mask such sales, keep them away from scrutiny, however he could.

He was insulated in the wealth from the street that unfolded as the car passed the town. The people there, with their little incomes, were jokes. How pathetic they seemed, in their drab clothes, so cheap! And if they knew how it was in circles they'd never penetrate! He liked it, in the company of the rich and influential to walk down soft carpets to the club, to drink with judges, politicians, directors. To these men England was one thing; the people at the bus stop hadn't even glimpsed that other world, didn't know of it. He exulted in his exclusivity. The heart pumped the blood under his clothes, he was alive, and his life was for the money.

The meeting was at ten, so he'd have to hurry to reach London by then. The city gave way to fields, then a smaller suburb with concrete residences near the road. The university - he looked to see if anyone was hitchhiking nearby. He'd like some soft sex if he could get some. He hadn't studied himself. There was no point in it. It didn't help you to get rich. And life was for the immediate luxuries like the dials on the dashboard, indices of speed and power, the expensive designer bag beside him on the front seat, the house he'd just left. He admired the business skill to make money any way; this was all. And official England was now this admiration; its government, its press, its respectable men, were committed to it. He smiled as the residences passed. He never opened a book. Now, television, that was different. Amusing. And it was nicer to watch the pictures. He felt at home to see how the luxury settings were always in; people liked to imagine these, how different they'd feel if they could own or have access to them. That was only healthy.

"You see, what we can do is sell the Security Company product with the car consignment. Then it's effectively cars shipped, and our documents prove it."

"As we did before, right?"

"Yes. That way if the opposition people hear of it, we're in the clear and so are the government bodies involved".

"Not that anyone cares much what we do, these days".

A laugh went up round the room; men smiled at each other, lit cigarettes. The government officials packed their cases, shook hands.

His wife opened the door to him when she heard the engine stop. He sat at his own oak table, to be served. The cutlery was silver, the meal correct in cordon bleu style. She'd met him when she'd been campaigning for the Young Conservatives and he'd been asked to give a lecture as a successful and coming businessman on the fringes of government. She'd been impressed by his spending power: that was the first affect he made. With him she'd be safe, never have to do anything. An immense, greedy laziness overcame her. Now, her life in the house consisted of anything she liked - a routine existed, not so varied, that suited her. He earned the money, talked things over with her; she looked after the house, kept herself attractive. It was a selfish world, with each looking after the self and giving in only in so far as it was politic.

They sat as usual to watch the news. The adverts comforted him; he knew he could buy whatever he saw. This was his self-ethic, to be able to buy. Buying was highest, so was money. The news came on. Dark skinned men stood with machine guns round an apartment block, police were beating other foreigners in a distant city, gas had been dropped to poison villagers. His wife passed round a chocolate, stood to pour coffee. How boring these foreign items were. There were more, nevertheless: men in camouflage uniforms chased a black man and began to beat him with batons against an armed Landrover. Somewhere else Arabs were being tortured. Together they sat, chewing the chocolates. His hand reached for hers, and they looked at each other, smiling. "I'll ring Jacksons about the home improvements tomorrow." She squeezed his hand in endorsement.

Containers suited him. In his trade it was better that what was swung on board ship wasn't seen. Not that the tourists at Southampton would care, in general, if the tanks, aircraft parts, military devices, were visible. After all, it was in all the papers, on the news, that money making, export was good. The money gained was the new sanction;

all was all right so long as money was gained. This then 'helped the country'. Exactly how it helped, to have business men in big houses, their accounts full for themselves alone, investment portfolios bursting, was obscure. Those who had most were best, the new altruists. Their selfish, rich lives helped everyone, so the credo ran.

Out in the desert, in the group of huts, the officers were waiting for the arrival of the trucks. The new interrogation equipment was expected soon. British made, in factories part-owned by the government and army, the equipment was of the latest design. It was in the British interest to support the right. The road curved across the hazy sand, and a convoy of lorries crept into view, on the horizon. The officers walked back inside, passing along the corridor where numerous small rooms led off on each side. All was ready for the new machines, and they went to tell the English technicians to be prepared to install the next day. A group of planes flew fast overhead, armed with the gases. English scientists would monitor the medical affects of the drop later.

It was the drinks party. Tables were set with small delicacies and the groups of establishment figures, businessmen, government people, chatted smartly. A few foreign dignitaries were present; they stood in expensive light suits, urbane, charming, bending to attend to brightly dressed women. Outside the English oaks in the long garden swayed in the breeze of the summer evening. The money had been made; the gathering was its symbol. A toast was drunk to the government, and a foreigner made a speech. The man in the white suit raised his glass. "You have helped us all. Now those subversives will see what we can do". There was a pause, then brief applause. The overt reference was not the British way to proceed, and there was later criticism of this breach in taste, laughter at the foreigner's expense.

The evening was over. The business man strolled with his dog down a dark avenue of shrubs and bushes. At

intervals white lights showed him the path. He was thinking things over. His money was increasing. From this deal
he could buy more shares, even get a controlling stake in
the armaments company. Thus the money gained from aid-
ing the extreme right abroad would pass on to finance the
right people here, in his own land. What else was there,
but this finance? He was oblivious of the night, the heavy
dark of the land joining the sky up ahead, the booming of
the wind above him. A pervert's greed drove him on, ob-
liviously adding up his assets, gloating. He had done especially well with the gas deal. He could do anything now,
anything. That judge, tonight, had told him how he'd let
off the upper types lightly, whatever they'd done: you had
to help your own. That was it - you had to, or disorder
reigned, the wrong sort got influence. He and his kind
would be in the right, for ever. This was the justice.

His wife was sitting reading when he returned. Her
book was a novel by a government minister, in which the
Soviet and artistic characters were all evil, sick, while the
British soldiers and businessmen had a monopoly of dig-
nity and honour. It was a convenient text for the times. She
looked ugly to him as she sat, and the urge to grip her face
with the palm of his hand, twist it about, came up in him
again.

"A nice party, darling". He smiled at her to mask his
dislike, putting on the genial, grey haired prosperous assurance he prided himself on being able to project at will.

"So nice to mix with the decent! I was so impressed by
Judge Twallin and his attitude. We must work together,
close ranks."

The businessman brushed his wife's forehead with his
lips. He wanted to bite out a mouth-sized piece of her
head, spit it across the room. Instead he squeezed her hand.
"Time for sleep. Separate beddies?"

'I think it's best, love'. The wife liked to lie alone,
where she could read magazines in peace. She'd never
really liked his bulk beside her; asleep he resembled the

shots of Brezhnev on his bier that had so frightened her a few years back - a high, barrelly chest and eyes dead and immobile, the frame rigid. Once she'd dreamed she'd been her husband's school teacher, spanking him with a sharp cane, harder and harder until the cane flayed up and down like a fast vibrating rod. She'd been ill, when she awoke.

In the market place the dusty cars stood in jams while the entrance to the bazaar was open, as of old, before the cars had come. The police were pulling along a young man, hitting him as they moved. A crowd watched, in silence. A heap of documents lay on the ground: 'the King's role in a cocaine ring. Workers murdered in mountain town.' The amateurish duplicated copies lay bedraggled. The policeman in his light uniform eyed the crowd. "You see what we think of such things". He began to unzip his trousers and a jet of yellow soaked the papers. "Pick one up if you want one". The other police stood by the meshed van, watching, laughing. Then the van was off, moving into the jam, insignificant, one vehicle among many. The prisoner would now disappear, as they headed to the desert.

The High Street was hot, and the tall London buses moved below the open window. Round a table sat swarthy men in jeans, open necked shirts, intelligent, as at a seminar. They were serious, worried. "You say the equipment came from here, England?" A man with thick glasses spoke.

"Bali, bali, yes - I saw it arrive. I was there. And English technicians are installing it, now."

"Who did the deal, this end?"

The men started to scrutinise documents, look at photographs. There was the businessmen, in his garden, the oaks framing a chair, the judge next to him. "These are the men".

The Englishman emerged from the bank, passed down the steps into the sunny street. All around rose the ugly blocks and buildings of other banks, investment companies, that also gained benefit from dealings such as his own. He knew he cut a smart figure, in the traditional business suit, like a successful man seen on television. His investments had doubled in value since the recent election victory of the right. All around was the city, where men like him were dominant. A smile of exultation came to his lips: what fools those other people were, if they had no joy in money!

In the club he sat in the brown leather chair, in the circle of men. The judge was smiling, in full flow, telling of a recent case. "You see it was quite clear the prostitute had told the truth. But I directed the jury to acquit the man." The others nodded, endorsing, attentive. "He had been, after all, high in the party". A minister smiled in approval, while a millionaire businessman called over a waiter to order drinks. "I hear your last dealings went well?" The minister quietly questioned the rich man, heard details of the deal, its shipment and safe arrival. "You see, the King is our man. He has to keep order, keep dissent at a minimum. In return we get oil, he buys our goods." A gust of laughter went up at an adjoining table where a professor of right wing philosophies was mimicking one of his students who'd queried the profit motive. "So quaint - such an earnest, ugly, little puritan. So out of touch." All was in order here; the like-minded exchanged information, influence, extended mutual patronages to acquaintances of each.

The judge and businessman were to dine together. The car was parked in a high rise block, not far away, below a bank in which both had controlling interests. Together they strolled in the evening sun along the street in which both felt they had more right to walk than anyone else. We are the rich, the ones in control; much of what happens in the world is down to us. The genial awareness ran in both heads. The car sped across the fields beyond the suburbs with the sun lightening the grass, the wind passing in undulations through the green. The men didn't look; the luxurious car seats, the blacked window glass, the courtesies of the driver, pleased them instead, and there were the

95

filofaxes to attend to, calls to make.

The table was set, the candles lit. It was the last course, and the judge was again mellowing into anecdote. The businessman's stupid-seeming face hung over his scraped bowl like a marred moon; the faces of the two wives were all attention, withered red lipsticked mouths in ovals of concentration, with all the physiological vessels below the skin, little brains pumping. "Just before", the Judge laughed, quickly, "Just before going into the studio the Prime Minister had told me the only concern was for the very rich! Oh, to see that broadcast! How the party was for everyone, helping even the pathetic fools at the lowest level!" The businessman laughed. "It's lucky for us they're all such fools. We can do what we like."

The coffee would be served with the news on, in the television room. Into every home in England, whether foul or damp, or extensive, luxurious, came these electric pictures and interpretations of world events, followed by a passive crime or comedy show. It was all picturesque and elsewhere. What horrible things those foreigners did to each other. In a distant land, today, women in black veils protested against a killing, tortures, arrests. In their turn, some were killed or arrested, on the screen. The businessman stirred his coffee, explaining with this background image why he'd chosen the kitchen design he'd shown the guests earlier. In his pocket, as he spoke, he could feel the pouch of white powder he was saving till later, as an after dinner pleasure for them all. "Such revolting people, over there!" The two wives were talking. "Aren't you just glad to be British!"

Quietly over the wall came the dark men, with long guns held in loose but alert grips. Their sisters, brothers, friends, were being arrested, shot, or interrogated with English sanction, tortured on English machines. They slipped past the security police sitting in a car at the front entrance, listening to cassettes. Inside the room, from the dark, they saw the coloured glow of the viewing set, the

96

backs of the viewers. It was easy, voluptuous, to smash the big window and aim the bullets. They were gone, swiftly, as the police emerged from the car, surprised by this residential intrusion. On the news later the foreigners were described as fanatics, murderers, while the judge and businessmen were men of decency and patriotism. The exported equipment functioned well in the foreign state, for the time being.

THE PERSIAN

She wondered, for a moment, why she had come. A broad and high window looked out on a drab lawn, closed in by a thick hedge, and other high blocks loomed beyond. It was raining, and long lines of drops ran down the pane. She was truly by herself, here, in the single room. A modern, wide bed provided with the room, and a small circular table of cheap white wood were the only furniture, while in the corner was a unit with a cooker and sink. The room didn't please her, though it was clean and modern. There was a sense of other lives clustered above and alongside, herself being on the lowest floor. She had come, of course, because of the disturbances in her own country, because she could study here, because this was Europe, Switzerland, not Iran, because....The reasons were easy to rehearse. But how to build a life here?

The thick wooden door, with the small peephole built in, she swung open. A few stairs ran into a wide marbled entrance area, where offices had display cases to advertise the products they dealt in. She passed these, bored and discouraged. A young couple were coming in the outer doors, ignoring her in a Swiss silence, as if intent on their own prosperity, polarising. She wasn't meant to be there. She couldn't care about their unstated disapproval; she didn't want to be in this Swiss town in any case. The road stretched past a deserted sports pitch, half flooded now, then bent slightly towards the nearby industrial estate, passing more high buildings with flats in. She would walk to the shops.

She'd been here six months now, walking each day alone along the drab, recent pavement to the nearby shops. Things were predictable. What she had seen of Swiss life repelled her. Nothing seemed to happen here, no-one flowed out to anyone, but moved in irritability, immune. Out here in the suburb, though, there were few people in the daytime; at night they were mostly in their apartments recovering from the wage labour. Maybe her feelings would change. She hoped so, now, as she moved down the road, out of connection, towards a café she knew. The place was deserted; she sat reading the paper in French. What she read discouraged her. The runways of the airport in her capital city had just been bombed, the western border threatened. She'd heard about these events the night before, lying alone in bed, in the dark, with her radio tuned to Iran. A flatness took her down as she read the confirmation, saw the photograph of the violated airport. She was cut off further from her family. Even if she'd wanted to return, she couldn't have got back now.

She was back, in her imagination, in the orchard of her grandparents. It was early in the morning before the sun grew strong. A low orange tree stood on a mound. She stared at it, relaxed, hopeful. At that age, just a teenager, she'd been ignorant of what was going on. Her father went to work, she lived in an apartment in the capital, part of her family. At weekends the family went to relations in the country. Now, she realised, her father must have played his part in the corrupt centre the city became. If corruption is everywhere, no-one is untouched. The business life could only proceed via bribes, defaults, contacts, keeping quiet about this and that. Her father had wanted the best, he'd claimed, and so had inevitably joined in the round of cheatings.

Anyway it was over. She wasn't there anymore. What was wrong with people, she wondered, that they would join in? She pushed the coffee cup away; the brown china was over familiar, the taste acrid, unpleasant. Things around her looked dark, her low spirits taking colour away. The small café, part of a shop, was neat and clean, dead. It was in this country, she knew, that many of the arms deals between the corrupt Persian King and ordnance firms had been fixed; here businessmen, the King himself, held accounts filled with criminally gained cash, kept secret. Now the rain was easing. She looked out at the grey road starting to gleam in the faint sunlight; it gave no sign that anything was amiss. Soon men would be driving home to eat lunch, then back to business. Nothing had been visibly transgressed; all was regular, complacent.

She would ride to town. There were no classes that day, so she'd miss no work. But lately it had been a struggle for her to attend the classes there were. A pointlessness was down on her. The bus slipped full along the wet roads. She felt crushed in, oppressed by the banal crowd. Her problems were invisible. What went on where she came from no-one cared about. Some countries were beyond the pale and hers was one. Switzerland, of course, in spite of its arms dealing connections and secret accounts for criminals and dictators, was never beyond the pale. A small-minded self interest seemed to fume around her as the roadway smoked in the emerged sun.

The town's preserved streets struck her as insipid, commercial merely. Every other shop seemed to be a jewellers. It was here rich Iranians had liked to come to load their fingers with rings. In adjacent shops expensive clothes hung. It was all miles away from her city of origin, just as she was now distant. But she didn't belong in this place either. The town lit up in the June sun, picturesque, with its medieval tower and stone steps with wooden roofs up to the restored cathedral, seemed a sham, like a shop display itself, a selling point. In this pretty context the deals were struck, the corruption had also taken place. No-one was much interested; in any case business was business and weapons had to be acquired somehow, illicit money banked. It might as well be here as elsewhere.

She wouldn't have looked very different to a smart woman anywhere. Her appearance gave little clue to her thoughts, feelings. She was well dressed, elegant. Her eyes, though, were screened off, slightly disconcerting. It was hard to tell her thoughts. She was reserved. In this mood no-one would approach.

An aimless urge made her sit in a café up a side street. It was meaningless, she decided, to be here, so she might as well waste time, hang around. The heat was building up. She sat on, puzzled about what was to come, what was possible. 'The churchmen back home wouldn't approve of me.' The thought made her feel estranged, doubly cut off. There was no real way back. In a bookshop opposite most titles would have been inadmissible for sale where she came from. Here - as few people read anything serious in any case - there wouldn't be a point to ban such texts. How could people get themselves into positions of such power that they could decree and ban this and that, as it suited them, establish social procedures to suit their own inclinations? The inclinations were, of course, set out as truths. Here in Europe it was the same, only the truths were different.

The day was hot and the street was full of people parading past dressed up, wanting to be looked at. In the town in summer there was an atmosphere of disintegration, people tight in their own presentations of themselves, looking for what they saw as pleasures. She was alienated as she sat, mirroring back the glances of the men, blank to them. Meanwhile her home country was disintegrating and where she sat also contributed to the break-up, this town so neat and well dressed. She wanted to break it up, rise from her seat and smash the bank windows opposite, knock the coffee cups off the tables from under the noses of the Swiss citizens. Instead she didn't get up, sat on there.

The weekend lay ahead, two tedious days of nothing. Sometimes she'd walk down to the lake where a tidy concrete quay provided mooring for expensive craft. The lake was small, but this didn't stop some Swiss from spending their francs on boats more suitable for the open sea. Unfriendly cafés lined the waterside, where waitresses took your money swiftly, pushing it down hard into leather pouches they wore slung round their waists. To pay was the zenith here; everything centred round the act of payment, or else being seen to have paid for something: clothes, a car, a boat. She hated the place. Back in Teheran there had been free and easy evenings with her family, dancing, joking. Nothing of that kind had come her way here. Perhaps it happened somewhere.

She wondered what she would do. Perhaps she would walk by the lake, yet again. She didn't want to meet anyone. No-one understood her feelings or reflections, her resistance to the cash spirit of this place. Maybe she would fly out to some other country. She had enough money. It would make her feel even more rootless, but - since it was actually the case now that she had no roots - what would this matter? She didn't want to see sights. The impulse was to get in motion, to be gone.

She was on the bus, going back to her room. A sense of failure was forming more and more solidly inside her. She had came here, to this place, and made nothing of it. Through the window she saw the residences of students, flats for other inhabitants, people walking. She was out of it all, in her own reality. The door slammed behind her, of the room. Outside the sun gleamed too intensely on the bland lawn, and there seemed nothing to do. The anger was rising in her, not to be beaten by this condition. She had tried to fight it for months. At first she had read, for example, sitting at the round plastic table in the evenings. But the context had overcome her gradually - the suburb all around, the sense of herself alone in a room. She couldn't understand why it had been like this. Back in Iran she had made friends easily, been at the centre of her circle. Here, though, she was neutralised, kept to a margin. Also she knew that the thoughts she had didn't made her accessible.

In the hot afternoon she took a familiar walk. You turned left after the entrance hall, passed up a road with flats on each side, then swung to the left up a steep hill, brief. After crossing a main road a lane led through an orchard. She liked this place, where the blossom hung white overhead, at Easter, and, what she had liked to see most, in the distance a line of hills marked the border with France. She could be gone, this place wasn't absolute. But it was all solitary. The walk continued past a trough used once for

105

horses to drink out of, now painted up and restored for the benefit of owners of new apartments in a converted farm, down a hill where expensive houses sat in their own gardens, and big cars stood in the hot road. To her right the lake glittered like blue poison in the distance. How she hated this place! There was a satisfaction in the complete opposition between herself and her environment also. The frustration of her life in Iran, the events there, fed into the dislike. How to express it all, release the emotion?

She couldn't stand the room. She was restless, back on the bus, to head for the station. She'd travel for the rest of the day, cross the land to Zurich. She liked to be in motion, to be somewhere that belonged to no-one, to be temporary. The train, suiting her, moved out of the shade of the roof, began to climb through terraced vineyards along the lake-side. There was the water, locked in between the hills. It looked unattractive, static, going nowhere.

This was the country her father had sent her to. He would pay for her to study at the university. In his mind the country had an attractive image of health clinics, fashion; he could tell his friends his daughter was there and impress them. It would also make it easier to leave his own land, if he had relatives elsewhere. The present regime was locking its people up, making entry and exit difficult. No-one had a free passage in or out any more. Her father seemed remote. It was herself, now, who had to pay the price of his vague decision. He went about his familiar business, followed routines. She'd wanted to go to England but hadn't been consulted. Now she was stuck here.

The train curved through a hot upland. She sat back in her seat, relieved to be out of the town although she'd be back in it again, she knew, in a few hours. Here her mind could fall aside, and she could relax. If a man sitting next to her swayed against her, she would enjoy that contact, momentary. But she didn't want to talk, make more contact. Her wish was to keep anonymous, not be bothered. She knew there could be no contact until she had resolved the friction that blocked her at her centre. Outside the landscape passed unnoticed, meaningless to her. She liked only the stations the train stopped at, with their transient purpose of departure, movement. At Zurich she knew she wouldn't walk in the city, but move about the station concourse, sit in a café she knew there, take the next train back. She liked it that the workers in the cafe were all foreigners like herself; people from Sri Lanka, Jugoslavia, used by the Swiss as menials. Outside the station ran the shopping street wives of her father's friends had praised, with its expensive clothes shops. She wouldn't go there. It all seemed like toyland, simple activities for adults who had failed to grow up, register anything. This was one basis of Swiss prosperity - a failure to grow up.

It was getting dark as the train wound down the lakeside, back to the town. She was half-asleep, bored at the prospect of the coming week. But she was also curious about how much she could withstand, where the boredom would take her. The experiences gave her a strength, of a kind: if she emerged from these she would know she could deal with anything. The emptiness itself was testing: just how out of contact can you get? Now she enjoyed the empty streets at the margin of evening and night, the rush of the taxi towards the suburb. When there were few people around at night the place was more bearable. She paid the driver, climbed the stairs and was again sealed into the room. She was tired, though, didn't need to stay conscious in it.

She had to get up early, to get to the classes. The university wasn't far away. It hadn't taken her long to realise that there was something deficient in the teachers she had encountered so far. She was studying English, and they compared unfavourably with those she'd had in Teheran. Some were Swiss, others English, here, and were filled with a conceit she could see no reason for. Once she'd been sitting having coffee in the restaurant and a man in a tweed jacket had approached her, smirkily. She recognised him as a pronunciation teacher. He sat down, uninvited.

"I bet you're glad to be out of Iran and somewhere decent, like Switzerland". She looked at him puzzled. "I'm from England", he went on, "but I find Switzerland just up my street". She didn't know what to reply. She finished her coffee quickly and left, leaving him looking after her, aggrieved. Another of her teachers, the Professor, gave lectures on the History of Language. He was a short man who often had traces of egg on his tie, also favouring a tweed jacket. He too seemed very pleased with himself. She found his lectures boring, and in the library one day came across a book, not by him, from which much of their substance and wording had been taken. She wondered, then, alone with her find, why Switzerland seemed so uninterested in choosing intelligent men for its university posts. If these two English men were representative, the course would be hardly worth following. The men earned big salaries, lived in luxury homes, were treated with unquestioned respect by Swiss citizens. There was also an upper Swiss Professor, she gathered, who'd written on the visits of Romantic poets to Lausanne; the book praised the lake highly and the town and the poems were scarcely referred to. All of these men she had observed eating in the restaurant, served by the Spanish waitresses on a special table, fussing over their food. Lunch seemed the highlight of their day. Another Professor, an American, was in a mental hospital.

She would have to submit. It was here her father had paid for her to study, so here she would study. Perhaps later she could change. She would bide her time. The small Professor, though, seemed to have taken a dislike to her. Once she had to consult him to obtain a statement she was studying to give to the police to get a residence permit. Although he must have dealt with other foreigners he acted as though her request was queer. "Of course, you've not been here long. How do I know you're in good faith? You're from where those mullahs run things. It's very different over here, you know. We like to be correct." He eyed her glintily through his spectacles, fingering a book on old English that lay on his desk, as if for show. "I'll look into it. You can go". He kept her waiting for two weeks or so, before the statement was handed over. It was late; the police had visited her meanwhile, finally placated.

The classes didn't satisfy her, neither did the place. She was nowhere, lodged in an inertia she couldn't get out of. She got up in her room, went to the classes, went home. A repudiating energy was in her, keeping others at bay. Letters came from Iran that pushed her spirits further down. Her parents weren't allowed to visit her. Back in Teheran everyone stayed indoors, uncertain about the squads of security men who patrolled the streets at night. She was living in two unreal worlds; this Swiss circumstance in which nothing much she liked took place, accidental, and the world she'd been brought up in, and had lived in actively until six months ago. The new reality should emerge elsewhere. It would soon be the summer break, and what should she do then?

She had addresses of contacts over in England. She wasn't much inclined to go, but the boredom of the room was a spur to get her out. She didn't expect anything. Her life had become flat, a withstanding. There was a system of routines, a few unimportant and brief contacts, and that was that. Again she crossed the deserted road towards the bus stop. How often she'd waited there, under the white steel shelter, fed her francs into the automatic machine for her ticket. No-one ever spoke. Across a car park where vehicles shone in the sun unpleasantly was a café. At first she'd thought that there some relaxed atmosphere might occur. But at breakfast time the place was full of tense working people, quickly drinking their coffee; at lunch time more people from work, eating in haste a three course meal. All was tense, joyless. She could be different, she believed, when she'd arrived. But the Swiss work routine drew everyone in, or else left you out. She was left out. She'd begun to miss classes believing she could learn more by reading books alone in the library.

She'd arrived. The bus from the English airport turned left onto the motorway, to head west. At least this place was different. There was more disorder here and people seemed more varied. In Switzerland she had felt cramped in by the mountains and cash spirit. As the bus ran in to her destination, though, her spirits fell. Here too were the restored houses, as if there was no new utterance to make and people had instead fallen back on past productions. And the past made money for you as show places, or contexts for your product or services.

The bus station was a mess of plastic signs, discarded cups, clots of people that struck her as ugly; men with pink legs in tight black shorts and with very short hair, fat women with fat children eating crisps and scattering bags on the ground when finished. She was used now to be factual, dismissive, to register what something really was. Long ago she had run out of the arguments with herself about tolerance and benefit of the doubt: people, things, were often ugly and hurt her. The papers on the plane over had described the gas used to blister the lungs of soldiers in the war - the death zone, over there, had no contact with these holiday people. She lived, herself, in part on the sandy strip where the missiles exploded and people she knew were killed. At the same time she was expected to enjoy herself, take her trivial studies seriously. An appetite for beauty sharpened in her. There could be beautiful things to see and feel somewhere. She was vague about what the beauty might consist of. It was better, she felt, to keep vague as so many desires came to nothing.

She walked up the holiday street with its rows of Georgian houses, most turned into restaurants or hotels. There were meant to be Roman remains somewhere. She stopped by a small park with a river beyond to look at a map her contact had sent her, to reach the flat. The town cheered her up now. She could be anonymous here, do as she chose. Maybe she would stay for ever. Anything was open, now the old ties were broken.

The streets were filled with people out, on holiday. Suddenly her mood was ebbing down again. The people in their summer clothes struck her as meaningless, bright like toys. With a shock she noticed two women in front of her. The nearest, with black curled hair was moving slowly, pushing a baby in a pram. From her loose movement, sensual, it was obvious she wasn't English. In front of the mother was a woman with light hair, expensive clothes, also foreign. Dull gold bracelets glimmered on her wrists. They were speaking Persian. She watched them, alert, as they moved on laughing, looking in the shop windows, casual but rich. She couldn't be like them, now. She felt shut out, doubly pushed aside, cheated of ease and pleasure. She went into a shop herself, and when she came out the women had gone. She wanted to see them, follow them. She hurried round a corner, but they weren't there. An unreasonable feeling came, of loss.

The Persians whose address she'd been given lived in the town centre in an elegant flat that overlooked an Eighteenth Century bridge with shops on it, and a weir below. All around the tourists moved, bright and aimless. The two men here were students. One was away, had flown to the States for his vacation to stay there in a community of Iranian friends in California. There, she knew, was even a television channel in Persian. America didn't attract her. The other man would be in and out, working as a chef now his studies were almost over, going at times up to London to visit his brothers. Now he handed her a key. She'd be left free, to do things with him or not. He was courteous, but looked ill, too thin. His own girlfriend had gone back to Teheran and couldn't get out again. Everything was in disorder.

The days passed, and a depression grew. One morning she got up early, just to sit in a café that overlooked a Roman bath. She was used to wasting time. Sometimes the man would join her and they'd talk of Iran, his situation

with the other girl. Both were united in desultory procedures, sitting there for hours, drinking coffee after coffee,
dispirited. There was some pleasure in the sense of waste.
Back in Iran the war proceeded, the morality squads patrolled the evening streets, picking up whoever they chose
for questions and worse. What went on in the English
town had that background for her. She was in no single
world.

The man was in London, the day before her return. She
sat alone in the darkened room on the shabby settee. Although the building in which the flat was had elegance,
the flat itself was cheap, furnished cheaply too. Being alone
and having no purpose was some fulfilment. It was as if
the breaking down society where she came from was pumping out a force that corroded her will, left her pointless.
But why should she have a point? In the hot darkened
room she could hear shouts of the visitors to the town
outside. She liked it best, now, inside. She sat neatly on the
settee, an attractive woman. She wanted to attract no-one.
It was better to be as she was, doing as she pleased, an-
swerable to no-one. The trouble was, she didn't want to do
anything. She liked to waste her time, herself, keep out of
contact. A breeze flapped the thick curtain, but the room
still stayed hot, half-dark.

She would soon be back in Switzerland, she knew, without having achieved anything here. Often it came back to
her, the image of the relaxed, elegant Iranian woman with
the baby and pushchair, and the other woman, probably a
younger sister. They had both been easy, abroad. What did
they care? They had achieved some happiness. In a way
she was sceptical of their picture that kept coming to her -
probably they bickered, were jealous gossips. But they could
also be happy. In her flatness, though, she knew she was
strong and could withstand what happened. One of the
Iranian men had returned a few days ago, and was full of
how in California the Iranians visited each other, kept up a
rich life of visits and pleasure. It didn't appeal to her, but

she registered how many of her nationality had left the actual land of Iran, and set up lives that kept up some of its customs elsewhere. But they were all definitely elsewhere, gone out.

Her Swiss room had no welcome for her. The taxi dropped her as it had so often before, in the yard outside the apartment block. The studies, such as they were, would start again the next day. Only, she had been astute enough to leave some projects open. She could, for example, work as a trainee dancer back in the English town. It appealed to her, the idea of working in the dance school. She could always read when it suited her, at home. The academic life, at least in the shape it took at the Swiss university, didn't attract her - nothing real seemed to be said, about the books, and the teachers seemed, so far, to have invested their interests elsewhere, in their Swiss salaries and the kinds of expensive housing they could afford. If what went on here was what studies meant, she wasn't interested. Elsewhere it could be better, of course, but she had no access there. Where she went she would often have to be present unofficially, clandestine. There wouldn't be a permit for her in England, for example. It suited her sense of her situation, to have to dodge and hide, unstable. She couldn't help this, nor the circumstances and events in Iran that had led up to the fact of her life now. She could get a room in the English town, lead her own life. It would cause problems with her family, but they were a long way off.

She opened the door, sat on the white plastic chair, leafed through the heap of advertising that had been put in her letter-box. The Swiss papers advised her to spend, 'profitez'. She would decide later. She'd do what she wanted. She felt released from the idea of having to please anyone. If things were socially broken, she'd please herself. It was a release, of a kind.

113

THE FINNISH SISTERS

It was now the girl placed herself in league with the poison sister. She would parade around the institute building, arm in arm, with a girl older than herself, skilled in drinking, sleeping out here and there, on people's floors, but all the time not really casual, with a man in the background, electric comforts in a safe flat. The friend dyed her hair white blonde, wore it bouffant style. She kept her own hair in odd tendrils, or else did it up into a tail that rose two more inches up above her head before hanging back from a wound round ribbon tied scruffily. Were they fools or not, pictures or not? They liked to keep people guessing, lure the men in and then leave them to hang, put them down. This was the youth.

She was split, pushed into this league, while another self, more positive, stayed frozen. Partly she wanted to be vile to anyone who liked her, or, worse, had an affect on her. Her own self-esteem was low, maybe because of excesses in the past, and this made her want to cut people down. In part, though, she believed she was better than anyone, the non-pareil. She did all she could to pique people, get them to take an interest in her. Then, when they'd extended themselves, she'd make fools of them. She was cut up, jagged, while she took care of her appearance, competitive, wanting to look the best, and her eyes still could look soft, even demure.

She'd invited the man to see a place she'd worked at when still at school. In the murky distance odd stacks rose up tall and thin - jets of white steam flushed out at intervals. A huge wall with a gate for lorries, like a port-cullis, blocked their entry to the works. All around spread the snow, and a few dark fir trees edged the approach road. The site was weird, there in the countryside, set in a wild, blank, scrappy landscape.

"They're mines - I did the cleaning in the offices. I had a boyfriend who lived here. So I spent time in the area, when I was at school." She looked like someone who had passed the point where having a boyfriend was interesting. A slightly poisonous self-deriding grin hung on her lips at

117

the memory. Behind the stacks the sky was turning purple black, like a cosmic bruise. She was beyond him in a sardonic, female mood he didn't grasp. She had stripped away romance, positive reaction to anything, to leave herself like acid. What she liked best was people who were alike bare.

"Do you ever read a book?" She looked surprised at the question.

"No - I don't get time. I'm more interested in photography." She liked it, to be out posing with her camera in her hands, to be in with the artistic crowd. The accent was American, though she was a Finn. She'd spent a year in the States as an au pair, drinking there, going to parties. He disliked her.

She took him back to her room in her parents' home. The low modern bungalow stood in deep snow along a road you could find in any Finnish town. All was monotonous uniform. Things in this country were largely to the same pattern. She showed him pictures of her best girl friend from school who now worked in Helsinki, four hundred miles south. Then she showed him photographs of herself as a baby. He wondered why she did all this, as she didn't like him.

"I always sat like that - so!" She puffed her cheeks out and pursed her lips, pointing to a plump baby girl in a smock sitting grumpily on a lawn. "I used to be good, until I was sixteen. Then my parents didn't know why I changed." Again the queer light came to her eyes, as of something lit up, sharp and vicious.

There'd been a famous band a few years back. She'd been singled out by the singer to be his girlfriend, a late teenage queen. Sometimes she'd run out on stage, requested by the band, to be there for the final song, in front of everyone. Somehow it had gone to her head. She saw herself as famous, one to be linked with the special. Only it had gone wrong, leaving her scornful, but always seeking another equal state.

"He used to come here. Everyone was jealous. They'd say, why should she have all that?" She smirked slightly, enjoying having antagonised the others. It was time to leave. They waited in the snow again for the bus to arrive. It was far below zero, too cold to be safely outside for long.

She had her own plans, friends in Helsinki, people to see. She would do exactly as she wanted. He waited for her to give some sign of friendship: stripped down, though, she was neutral, ambiguous, not committing herself to any direction or procedure. She might work briefly in a hotel; he could 'drop by' there, in the capital, she told him, if he was passing through. A partial contempt for men occupied her. She didn't need anyone.

This man, she thought, in merely liking her hung a heaviness on her she disliked. She wanted to be out, casual, free. This was her code. No man should encroach on her. Nothing should carry her away. She could drink to oblivion, flirt with men, even sleep with them, but it came to nothing, left her emptier and more cynical. She would look after herself, take what she wanted and leave the rest. She thought in terms of rock songs, rock musicians, the fantasy of low key relaxed behaviour, seeing through everything and taking refuge in drinks. Nothing was worth doing. The attitude had been confirmed in the States. Only money and appearance counted; anything else was shit.

The band bus loomed round the corner, She'd arranged to travel down to the capital with the musicians. She knew people like that since she'd been the singer's girlfriend. Only now she kept aloof from men. She'd seen them sleeping through the alphabet of girls' names on tour, and though she'd joined in at first now she was left cold. In fact the joining in had made her cold, blasé. Nothing really mattered much. What gave her most pleasure was to get men interested in her and then to cut them off.

The men were pleased enough to have her on board the tattered vehicle. They weren't in the first rank of bands, but had been a few years back. She was one of them, one of

119

the boys. Sexual difference had no secrets. All were really the same, men and women. Each was out for himself or herself, each had a certain number of thoughts, ideas, a certain range in which gratification was to be sought. There were no mysteries. All was minimal, low, things were worthless or meaningless. If any difference between the sexes did, nonetheless, come up, it was to be ridiculed, jeered at. Partly she wanted to be a boy. Her vacation passed.

He rang her when he got back. The number sounded out. A blurred voice answered. Maybe she was drunk, or had been making love. It was all possible, even likely.

"I guess it's the wrong time to ring." She was silent. "Busy this weekend?"

"No, I'm not busy. But I'm not going anywhere. Later I'll do something. I don't know when. I want to be by myself." She spoke determinedly. There was a depressed resistance in her. The call was over.

She liked it, to be cold in her image, to patrol with her girl friend, crystal sisters on parade, apart. The phone call meant nothing to her. She wanted to deal out pain. When she was made up, and pulled on her oddly elegant clothes, her pointed black shoes with the half high heels - awkward to walk on ice in these - she exceeded the rest, tall, striking, intact. She had a curious off-hand style. She might wear jeans bought second-hand from a Helsinki dock-side stall, with an expensive dark-blue jacket, or else loose flowery trousers and a pullover she'd knitted herself. She wanted to stay intact, but break into others' intactness. She filled out with desires to jerk and cut; to look good made the cutting more of a thrill, like a dandy operating a torture machine, and sitting elegant afterwards. Her women friends encouraged her in this.

She was gone, ahead, stepping out with her friend, two attractive women. They would go to sit in some bar, see who would approach, ridicule them on the spot, or later. They would talk to each other, two women together, theorise. Later one would ring the other and they'd talk about their experiences. One would have found herself at home, four hours drive away, with no recollection of how she'd got there, who she'd been with. But a main component of the bar dialogue would be to attract men and put them down.

He was walking alone in the night along an icy causeway. It stretched ahead, the traffic lanes empty at this time. Suddenly he recalled an excavated field like a quarry he'd once had to pass in Germany on his way to work. Each day the hollow was filled with more and more bags of rubbish, coloured differently, reds, blues, blacks, yellows. The waste that spilled out was all in metallic or rubbery coils, shiny or sponge foam, pointless. The whole was a random chaos of sickly coloured items, mixed together to be buried in earth. This was like peoples' lives.

The women swung on, bright, steeled up, to the bars. He was out of it all, gone his own way, as they'd gone theirs. Contacts were all flung out, centripetal: each against each, woman against man. There was no warm coming together.

The causeway was slippery with ice. The thin moon beat above, casting its harsh glow on the tree branches, making the roofs reflect its cold white separating light.

THE ESCAPE

Her father was standing in the hall as she put her key in the security lock. He looked at her quizzically as she came in, eyeing his watch. He had been waiting there, to check her.

"Your courses get later and later. It's seven fifteen. Let's hope you're learning something." He smiled, not altogether pleasantly. It had been a difficult day, negotiating, seeing prospective contractors, then at the oil company, monitoring accounts at the Teheran office. His daughter looked back at him; what had she returned to, that made her feel she must do this and that on its behalf? The apartment itself seemed still, unloving. But she was used to it, and had arranged her own procedures there. Through the rain covered window she could quickly see the familiar building plots opposite, where further blocks of luxury flats were to be put up. Her father owned half the block she looked out from.

Her mother emerged from her bedroom, smoothing down an Armani skirt she'd just put on.

"Come, come, she's been seeing her girlfriends, chatting. The girl's got to live!" The father moved off to get ready. Tonight was the meal with his colleague. Jali had forgotten, and now she had to hurry to prepare herself. Her mother came to her room, as she changed.

"Jali". The tone was interrogative. "I met Mrs. Bazargan this morning. She told me she saw you in the street with a man. Who was he?" The daughter controlled her instinctive tendency to shake. She had to think quickly, and told the truth. "He was one of our new teachers. He asked me about my marks." The mother eyed her suspiciously, the lipsticked mouth, elegant, curving into a sneer. "You're not being a little bitch, are you?" Suddenly, with a glittering crack of bracelet, the sharp red nails outward, her palm crashed hard against her daughter's cheek. "Don't talk to men in the street. Now you've given Mrs. Bazargan a meal to gossip about." Her mother turned, walked haughtily on high heels to the door. Her hair was coiffed upwards like the women's on the television quiz programme to mark the

125

Shah's celebration; jewels hung below her ears, gold against her brown skin.

Jali's sister came to stand in the hall-way. The two sisters stood there silent, waiting for the black limousine and driver. Their mother was also silent, stern-lipped, behind. Now she wouldn't speak to her daughters for a day or so. Tarane glanced in sympathy at her sister. She was more resilient, detached from the family, absorbed in her political studies. She saw the futility of direct challenge in the home. Her parents could cut off her money to study, force her to be a secretary, like her mother at the National Oil Company. Tactically, that evening, she set out to be especially sweet to her father, to ally him with them.

He appeared now, coming down the stairs in his black suit, imposing in his squat breadth. He eyed his daughters in appreciation. They looked attractive, good girls. He took in his wife's mood at once. He was used to her shows of temperament. He put his hands on both girls' shoulders. Each, in spite of herself, felt the blood bond, daughter and father, run in her veins. The car drew up. The family climbed in, prosperous seeming, externally harmonised, each member smart, fulfilling his and her duty in the family group. But in Jali a lonely hatred was welling up, against her mother. She had to shut it down, dissemble.

Mr. Gharlou was sipping from his glass, stately on the settee, while his colleague sat neatly beside him, drinking brandy. They were discussing oil prices while their wives talked in the kitchen. The two girls had been left at the table, in another room, with the two sons of Mr. Karajan. The boys sat at leisure, their dark hair neatly styled. The oldest, about twenty six, was playing with his silver fruit knife, smiling at Jali. He liked the girl, wanted her.

"I'm going to squash tomorrow. You want to come? We can take my father's Jaguar, go to a film afterwards."

Jali stared at him. "What about your job?"

"No problem. I'll tell my father at the bank, and he'll give me time off."

126

"No, I don't want to come." He turned up his eyes, straightened the sleeve of his expensive sweater, flicked ash off his cigarette. "And you, Tarane?"

"No thank you. I have to go to a political meeting at the university." The man smiled, sardonic, grinned at his brother, a year younger than himself. Both were used to such skirmishes, and didn't take the rebuffs too absolutely. Wherever they went they approached women in these ways. Now the younger man spoke.

"You're too serious, you two. We should enjoy ourselves. Live well, keep happy. You know?"

"Enjoyment! That's all you think of, isn't it. Clubs, dancing. Why don't you grow up?" Tarane was scornful. The men smiled back, cool with her. In answer, one pulled out a pouch of white powder, sniffed it up from a tiny mirror, passed it to his brother. The girls watched, indifferent. Smiles grew on the men's faces. The door opened, and Gharlou and Karajan strolled in, arm in arm.

"Go on, get to know each other. Let's have dancing." Karajan moved across to put on a cassette of disco music. Gharlou, sterner, detained his arm. "No, we must go soon. So no dancing - this time. Perhaps later." He smiled across at his girls.

It was time to leave. In the car no-one spoke, at first. Mrs. Gharlou was still proving her silent displeasure to her daughters, while her husband was nevertheless in a good mood. He had received information, addresses of contacts, that would help him advance.

"Why so serious? Life is good, let's live it." He turned to Jali and Tarane. "They're nice boys, smart, well-mannered. That eldest boy, he's very promising, at the bank. He's a Doctor of Business, too, American University." His daughters sat, neutral.

"They're a little wild, the boys, perhaps," the mother proposed, drawn in.

"No, nothing like that," Gharlou rejoined. "They need to be sociable, it's useful in business. They're just young.

True Persians, a good family. You're too choosy." Nothing direct was being said, but the girls both felt something was being set up. From time to time their father did such things, organised events where young men were, to fulfil what he saw as a father's duties.

She sat in her room with her objects around her. What was to be done? The whole place depressed her, but it was what she was most familiar with. Outside the thick curtains lay the city; she went each day to study, saw friends, came home. Obstructions lay around her; now she would sleep her way out of them.

Tarane was walking beside the high railings of the ministries that were sited near the university. Trees grew in gardens here, and elegant old buildings built a long time ago by the British stood at a distance from the crowded, snowy road. Armed guards stood also at entrances, and black limousines waited in lines in the road. She paused, to see the flag of the United States hanging from the chrome rod on the first car's bonnet, the circular disc of the German Economic Research Unit on another car's number-plate. She was late for her lecture.

Inside the courtyard of her college though, things were different. Huge handwritten sheets of paper hung from the high enclosing railings, and angry groups of students were talking, shouting. She joined some people she knew, listening to another student addressing a small meeting. "They were just walking, the Trade Union people, along the motorway from Karaj. Just poor people, illiterate. Then the army came and shot them down, all thirty of them." She took an interest in such incidents. They were increasing. The brothers of several girls in her college had been arrested on random charges - there were rumours of torture, being heated and burned on an electric element rack. She didn't know what to believe. Back in England, where she'd studied English one summer, she recalled how she'd read about her king in an English woman's magazine; pictures showed him urbane and kindly, enjoying fast motorbike

128

rides on his estates, dedicated to the new Iranian civilisation he was building. His wife was the benefactress of hospitals, schools, charities, the English readers were informed.

There were shouts from across the road. "The Americans train our Secret Police and torture squads. The English sell us tanks!" A group of men in balaclavas and ragged clothes were racing towards the limousines, cringing as they ran. Before they could get near an armoured car bore down on them and they were truncheoned aboard. The captives were swarthy, poor looking. The students looked on. Such events weren't uncommon.

At home Jali was sitting again in the living room. Her mother was out, working at the oil ministry with her father. She had come home, cutting short her own activities, in order to be on time, to find no-one else in. It was exactly seven. The room was separate from the outside world - there was little worth seeing from its windows, just a dusty road now snowed over, more blocks, and the elevated motorway in the distance. Inside, a heavy oak cupboard with glass windows revealed dolls, crystal glasses, photographs. She felt tense, empty, over-familiar with it all. The phone rang.

"Hello, my darling, my cherry. We will be later tonight. We must eat with your uncle. You eat with your sister. We will come at nine."

She need not have hurried. The familiar voice recalled her to her organised life as a daughter. She took an orange from a silver bowl on the dark mahogany table, sat looking out at the stretch of wasteland opposite, where the foundations of the new blocks had been laid.

She heard the car pull up below, the click of the doors being opened by the chauffeur, the key in the security lock of the flat. The big man was in the room, stout and dark, his fierce face now softened in smiles. He looked aggressive, his coloured shirt open at the collar, his jacket stretching on powerful shoulders, the large stomach swelling un-

129

der his shirt as he took off his coat. His wife and Tarane followed him in; the mother pulled off her fur coat, shaking out her hair with a deft hand movement. She disappeared towards the kitchen to supervise the servant.

"My daughters!" He advanced jovial, grinning, the master of the family. Jali looked up from her book, smiling back, nervous, anticipating a rebuke. But no, he was easy, shaking her jokingly by the hand, winking and handing over a present of pistachio nuts he'd bought her. He was then gone, into the bedroom, to emerge in his pyjamas, slippers. Jali knew he would now sit on the long leather settee, watch television, drink tea. The routine was familiar. On each side of the television hung religious texts, suspended from the wall like pictures; various photographs of his mother - an old woman swathed in black - his wedding, were displayed in silver cases about the room. His presence filled up the place; he was the largest person there. Jali's mother came in with a tray of glasses, tea. He put a cube of sugar in his mouth then drank, in the manner of country people. All his family were about him. The wife withdrew, to rest. She rested often, and when not resting, queer frustrations would seize her, impulses to be viper-like. The rest of the time she could be charming, even kind.

The television showed American built jets, flying in on delivery for the Iranian Air Force, the Shah shaking hands in the U.S.A. with its President, sealing the deal.

"It's good for business, these links with the U.S." He turned to Tarane. "You see, you students, you're wrong to be against those planes. There are many outside against the King. He must defend himself."

"But most people here can't write." Tarane flared up, in spite of herself. "There aren't enough doctors. He should spend money first on these things." The father turned, smiling, to his daughter.

"He will. You'll see. Right now he's just making his position strong. And it's not so important, reading, writing. My men can't do either, but they can work well." He was secure in his world of developing prosperity. Tarane knew better than to argue with her father. The evening dwindled away. The girls sat on, silently, near their father while he watched the news. At the first opportunity Jali moved off to her room. This was how it always was. She had to choose the right time to do what she wanted, adjust herself in cunning to the outer scheme. Tarane would follow when she also could.

The two girls sat in the half-lit room. A green curtain blocked the window. Outside it was snowing, but inside there was warmth, luxury. A few religious texts had been hung by the father on the walls.

"It gets worse, the system gets worse. More people shot. And the money goes to people like Bazargan and his boys."

Jali looked at her sister briefly, then said abruptly, "He's coming - this month." Tarane smiled and went to put her arms round her sister. "You really do want him to come." Her tone wasn't questioning, but endorsing, emphatic.

"Yes, of course. Then I have what I want."

"I'm glad."

The sisters paused, stopped speaking. It was time for Tarane to pray. She was dutiful in this respect. She liked the old Islamic decorations, the pale blues of ancient mosque tiles. From her view of religion a sense of justice, already strong, was intensified. She looked round, after her prayers, at the pictures.

"Why do they put the Shah next to the holy texts? The Shah is a murderer, a torturer." Jali watched her sister turn the King's face to the wall.

"Our father will be angry." Tarane was referring to the foreign man's arrival. Jali shrugged. "He need not know." She had already planned to sub-let a flat for him. She was practical in her schemes. But she was also uneasy. To be secretive put a stress on her, divided her.

Her father was calling from the living room. He was waving the phone in her direction. He smiled, genial. "It's the Sayd Bazargan boy. He was ringing me on business.

He wants to speak to you." Her father sat close to the phone, supervising the call. Jali could hear music from the restaurant the other end, imagine Sayd immaculate in his suit, bought in Italy on one of his European shopping excursions. She disliked the man. He was obsequious, concerned, trying to charm her round. They spoke a few polite phrases and she gave the phone back to her father. He imagined he had done her a favour. She went back to her room, irritated. How to be out of it all?

The music was up, at the club. Down cleanly carpeted halls where large mirrors in gold painted frames hung on walls, the young men passed to the tables. Women in clothes from European shops sat there also. A few people were already dancing. Most of these people had been out of Iran, to study, or merely to travel and shop. All was for pleasure, enjoyment. Why not? They carried it off well, these people, drinking and dancing. Who cared about the rest? Life was good, why not use it to enjoy? The girl, Jali, was forgotten as Sayd approached a table of friends. He didn't care about anyone. A licentious atmosphere in which anything was allowed and possible burned out of the candles on the tables, the music that played, the glow of the ornaments, the peoples' moods. A physical warmth in which problems were forgotten was set up. The Bazargan boys liked to gamble: it was easy, over at the roulette table, made in London its green baize claimed, to lose and win the dinars, place the counters on the numbered squares, be caught up in the glittery spinning of the wheel.

After the call Jali sat, to think. She wouldn't mind dressing up, going to a club, just for herself. Only her father wouldn't allow it: "When you're married you can go." Nevertheless she had managed to go at times. She liked the display, the luxury context, but mostly she liked the neutrality, the fact these places were not home and nothing was expected of her in them. She was sick of rules and being controlled. She didn't like Sayd. But here you had to use men as the means to enter this and that, otherwise nothing was accessible. Her father had even decided what she and her sister could study.

She was back with the man who was coming, walking in the night in the grounds of the English mansion where the school had been. Soon he would be there, in Teheran. The contact lingered in her, changing her. She didn't want to go out, but wait for him. A romance bore her up, but didn't take her in advance into difficulties that might arise. They would solve them, in any case. It was as if with him an extra dimension had been created in which luck ran their way. Secluded in the remote countryside they had made their own world. It could still be like that, she had decided. Her father wouldn't have more power, he would dwindle. Partly it disturbed her, as if he would deflate to nothing, leave her exposed to choices she had no experience of making, a foreigner in her home land. She wanted to pierce him, have herself to herself.

In the morning she went out. The streets were quiet in the rain, ominous. At street corners groups of unemployed men gathered, unshaven, in cheap jackets and flared trousers. A few tanks ran the length of the main street, sandwiched in between cars and buses. A tension hung over the city, that was emptier than usual. She waited for a taxi in the gutter at the roadside, squashed into the orange car that took several passengers along a fixed route, like a bus. She wanted to get home after her classes. A cloud of black haze hung over the business suburbs round the bazaar, and she could hear sirens. The taxi driver raised his hands on the wheel, banged them down. "All day - diversions, streets closed. They say the King is going, the airport will be closed too. No-one knows what will happen."

Everything was breaking down; she pulled her coat tighter around her, feeling alone. How would it affect her and the man? But there had been disturbances before; tensions built up, exploded in riots, shootings, then all went back to how it had been.

They took the gravel path from the white door of the

Georgian house, paused by the bushes that swelled raggedly and unkempt into the driveway, then walked on into the hot night. Now she remembered this as she climbed the stairs to the apartment. She would like to be back there in the peace of the country lane. Instead she was trapped among these frictions. The servant was preparing rice; Jali put on a cassette of Persian music, looked round the room. It all meant nothing: the expensive, heavy settees, the glass cabinets, the long table where so many meals had taken place. Perhaps the man wouldn't come for her, and all would drift on as before. But no, she was sure of him. She had her studies, but these didn't signify much. The richest students often did best, as it was the fathers of these who could pay teachers' bribes. There was no procedure she knew that money didn't intervene in. Only in the family, its visits to relatives, its parties, was she safe from the need to be wary of money interest. The city was constructed out of a network of corrupt interests, individual and international, and she was meant to create a life among them. The expected way was to marry a rich man and be bought clear of the confusion and discomfort the less rich were forced to endure.

She was back in her old room in the house in the English countryside. An energy passed up into the secluded spot, that was alien to her, She hadn't been used, at first, to the big trees that hung branches outside her window, or the lawn below, not very neatly kept up; which ran to some bushes along a wooden fence with fields beyond, the nearest once part of the estate. But gradually she had got used to the green landscape around, the occasional trip to the town a few miles off, at weekends. She had been there a few months before; now in Teheran, it was as if she had never been there, except for the man she'd met. The world her father lived in had no connection, except in business terms, with England. She'd been able to drive out at midnight, anytime, with the man, talk to him about anything.

Now she wondered why she was bringing him here to

that strange place, her own country - except it seemed it was a natural continuation of what had begun. It only vaguely occurred to her that the context might alter the flow between them, started as it had been in her freedom of movement. Here, where she was expected to be in by seven in the evening, to give a full account of her activities, things would be different. You had to live all on different levels, move back and forth, from emotional line to line, negotiate different peoples' restraints, be in diverging societies all at once. It was tricky, it seemed to her. Already she had gone beyond her father's range of experience, and yet he was in charge of her, in Iranian terms. It was no good turning to her mother who envied the younger woman her freedoms and urges, was caught up in vanities of her own.

It wasn't clear to her, as she sat, whether the man would come or not. The country might be sealed off, an enemy might attack. Things were volatile, in vicious flux. Everything was unstable, bar the sense of what it had been like, for her, back in England. She was with him, waiting in the heat on a small country station, with tall, still trees opposite, just to watch the trains pass in the night. There had been a world about them that was only theirs, not subject to any rules. They could come and go as they pleased.

The next day the weekly family party took place. Early the chauffeur waited in the snow edged road below the half finished blocks. The hollow red bricks jutted into the white, crude. Jali's mother in a black fur settled in the back of the American car, chic, unmotherly, potent with friction and dissatisfaction. Beside her was Tarane, subdued, submitting. The father sat in the front, in a business overcoat he'd bought in London, his skull beneath the greying black hair hard and stubborn from the rear. There had been reports on the news of troubles on the Iraq border, some movements in France around a religious leader they knew little about. This was on a foreign broadcast the father had heard, to check the gossip at work. The suburbs were deserted as they passed - the guards waited in the sweeping entrance to the King's palace, but the King was away, the blinds were down in the villas. They didn't pass any poor quarters, which were on the opposite side of the city.

The hills rose round them, cupping them in, and the road narrowed. The day was clear, with a wintry brightness that made the distant mountains loom up clear edged. The grandmother's house was in farming country; her husband had been a landowning lord, feudal in his area. The car swung down a side road, the long wide bonnet pointing blunt towards the house at the end, modern and extensive. An old woman in a black chador moved to meet them. Jali felt a surge of repugnance for the half bent dark figure, the religious scripts behind, framed in the hall. She was expected to follow a routine of respect. Drearily she rehearsed it - the servants would bring out the rice, set it on a long oak table, the meal would begin. Other relatives would call. She would go with her sister to listen to tapes of Persian music in a side room. There might be television. Then the ride home would follow, as before. She was at a distance from it all. What had happened in England was more real, and present. Her grandmother twisted towards her, pressing food on her, asking about her studies, her marks. Meanwhile her father's eyes were also on her, monitoring for defects in response. Her mother was carrying on a half-flirty conversation with a business colleague. How Jali hated them all. But she kept up a shiny, outer self, smiling back at the old lady, giving details of her week's lectures.

In the dark, the wild landscape threatened the car. On the edge of the city lights were on at the air-base, and she could see fighter planes fuelling up, men on parade. Anything could happen here. She knew that a point of excess had been reached that meant all things were possible. The Government could do anything in reaction to opponents; opponents could do anything in their anger. A limit had been passed beyond which any cruelty might be dealt. Her father had done well under the present regime. Now he would have to steer carefully to adjust to any new one that might occur.

Where was her personal self in all this? She turned again to her memories of the man, recalling his touch and hers. He should come soon, before the country was closed down in war.

"You are silent, Jali. You are not like our daughter tonight." Her father pressed her. "It was nice that Mr. Bazargan called today. We can eat with him again. But next week his sons will be in Italy, so we will call the week after. They have gone for shopping." He lowered his voice, indulgently. "They know how to enjoy life."

His wife cut in. "And they are so Persian, they are like family already."

"Maybe they are like your family." Tarane broke in, the friction between them all issuing in her words. In the dark car her mother hissed in breath, and with long red nails dug a pinch into her daughter's cheek.

The mother was keeping watch, days later. She moved among the crowds in the unfamiliar suburb, where poorer people lived. Up an alleyway she saw the glowing fires of the bakers' booths, cages with goats and chickens for sale. A friend of her husband had rung her, to say he had seen her daughter in the city with a man. Now she would loiter in the area, perhaps to catch Jali out. She would like to find outlet for a rage that had been accumulating. Partly the fury was social, spreading in from everyone outside, partly a reaction to her own bright role as wife of the rich businessman, an anger at herself for becoming empty. She wanted to cut out with her red nails, see others and perhaps herself, bleed. Now she had errands in the area, so she could combine these with the search.

The pavements were crowded, but people moved aside, even standing in the open drains along the damaged road surface to let her by. Army officers in thick long overcoats from a nearby barracks glanced at her in approval. She was chic, a product of the regime. A network of alleys opened out to her left; a squat man, bulky, sat in the road in an armchair, while his workmen loaded a pick-up truck with lengths of iced up building wood. There was no sign of her daughter. She ordered meat from a merchant, caught a taxi home. Only she had been alerted now, and would keep watch. But perhaps the man had been mistaken. She was confused. It wouldn't be the first time a malicious story about Jali had been sent. The men often invented such stories after being rebuffed by the girl. But she always kept watch, just in case.

Suddenly, it wasn't easy to go out anymore. The mother found herself more and more confined to the apartment. Once she had been caught up in a knot of wildly protesting men, jostled, pushed into the gutter, jeered at as a Shah's doll. People she hadn't seen before, in rags, suddenly appeared in squads outside the fashion boutiques and restaurants, pointing and shouting. Her daughters were better at negotiating the new conditions than she was, dodging down back streets, evading the areas of fighting.

Jali wanted to be gone. More and more it seemed to her there was no point in the man coming. Events in the city were becoming daily more tense, bizarre. One morning she'd found it impossible to pass along the main street, because of demonstrators. The university was closed altogether, after a period of being surrounded by armed soldiers as classes went on. There was wild talk of communist students taking over, a greater role for the church. Foreigners were frequently attacked by gangs of zealots. She knew many foreigners were in Iran just to make money out of it, so the attacks in themselves didn't bother her. It all meant, though, that it would be a difficult time for a foreigner to arrive. Her personal self seemed to be slowing up, seizing like the city itself. Tarane was out, often, now at political meetings. Her boyfriend, a teacher in a country district, had disappeared, put into custody for security reasons after expounding Tolstoy's essays to his classes. Any-

138

one suspect was being rounded up. The city was friable, separating into groups of mutual hatred.

Now Jali knew she had to be cunning. It was plain the man couldn't come - she would have to go to him. Some pretext must be found, to convince her father she had to leave. He was rarely at home, struggling to adapt at his work to new regulations, alignments. The Oil Ministry was closed; new men would be appointed when it re-opened. His own business remained: building. As food shortages were expected, he could perhaps move into deep freezing in addition. He would sit gloomily watching television news, consult with groups of friends in the lounge. His assurance was diminished. Jali would see the men standing, reaching absently for nuts, on the glowing Chinese carpets, as she came and went from her room. Her mother often lay down all evening with headaches, fits of nerves. The life as they'd known it was broken, the family was loosening inside the social break.

She would sit looking out of her window at the fiery flares in parts of the city, hear the crack of guns. Once she saw a man pulled from his limousine, laid out in the gutter, his face kicked and spat on. She didn't care. Probably he had been a torturer, the King's agent, or a self-enclosed moneymaker. In the sky the small moon beat out its white gleam, shining queerly on the deserted asphalt of the road. This place was meaningless now. She wanted to go where she wasn't exposed to daily hate and friction. There was good cause for the hate, but, personally, she didn't want to be caught up in it. Bleak revelations came daily - the former Justice Minister had dealt in cocaine and weapons, a female relative of the King had enjoyed watching prisoners whipped, even executed. Once off, the social lid revealed varied disintegrations. She was drawn in. Perhaps she wanted just comfort, to be paid for by her father, loved by him. This was one motive. She watched a thin cat spring onto the half-built wall opposite, creep along the uneven top, silent, looking for ease. All the time she was conscious of her mother lying sick next door, on the luxury bed, given up to helplessness. Tarane was out for long hours, putting up posters, demonstrating, To leave seemed like abandoning everyone, being a traitor, but staying meant to go passive, give up, be undermined and controlled.

The man had written that he had a job in Switzerland. She could go there. She kept it as a hope, secret from the others. Somehow she must get out. Her father sat bent over his plate at breakfast. He eyed her mournfully. "Well - my cherry. It's good you are here with us." Her spirits sank. But she knew she had to persist.

"Yes, but my education. They don't know when the universities will open again. I could go to study outside Iran."

The older man looked at her, in appraisal. It was no more than he had been thinking to himself, earlier. Besides, a bridgehead outside the country could be useful. The whole family might have to leave. He told her he'd think it over, talk to relatives. Everything was different now.

The big jet was dropping towards the Swiss city. The man would soon be waiting for her down below. She was out, but in part she felt bereft, caught up in the events she'd left behind. What would come was unfixed, uncertain, new. This excited her. She was glad the old systems had broken, and let her emerge,to build a new form. The man too was abroad, and they would both be foreigners, loose. She didn't have many hopes of Swiss life, but they could move on, not fix down in any particular social shape. She knew, in any case, that the Swiss had abetted the corrupt regime, banking its money, mediating in its weapons deals, hiding the drug profits of ministers and officials in secret accounts. The disease had needed foreign collusion to take hold. Now they should use the systems for their own survival, without ever giving their endorsement. Who knew where they would end up - she didn't care.

She saw again the powdery white dust rising up off the

drive to the country house as the taxi had left at the end of her course, swishing against the English bushes as it passed. The fields had spread down to a canal and a railway, overlooked by the tall windows of the mansion. In the heat the fields had looked whitish green, the broad-leaved trees had been welcome to walk under, with the man. It was perhaps risky to trust the touch between herself and him merely. Again, she didn't care. Why not take risks?

He would arrive an hour later than her flight. She sat at a counter drinking coffee, her black hair brushed finely to her shoulders, her legs crossed elegantly in a shortish skirt. If she looked rich, she also looked thoughtful now. This place was peaceful; a great weight of tension was lifting. At the airport in Teheran the officials had kept her for hours, re-examining her documents, searching her cases, keeping things awkward, insulting. She had to bribe hard, to get through at all. Here no-one bothered her, apart from a few stares from Swiss businessmen, on the look-out for women. These were easy to deal with, trivial in the context of the trials she'd been undergoing. She realised the huge distance between herself and these Swiss citizens, because of her recent experience. They were unlikely to see their own context burst open and revealed, on a wide scale. They seemed to her limited, unaware.

At last she saw him moving through the crowd, his eyes turned towards her. Laughing, she moved from her stool to greet him.

The Ministers

It was a high window - too high, really, to see closely what was happening on the ground. The minister stood, looking out, speculating. His assistant waited in deference. "You see", the minister was friendly, confiding, "We cannot improve their conditions. We don't want to. And besides, are they really so bad?" The assistant consulted some papers, suave as he opened his executive case. "Our sources say they're close to riot. There's been more trouble in that suburb than any other."

The minister looked disturbed. The Prime Minister had instructed him to prevent riots. He was failing. An attendant brought in a silver tray with silver covered plates. His mind was back, momentarily, at Oxford, undergraduate days, the debating society and Conservative Club, motoring down at weekends to Cirencester for the polo. It had been an easy time, without much study, with his own people around him. Now everything was so much trouble. He nodded to the assistant to leave him. With a petulant, effeminate movement he stuck out a thin suited arm to lift the lids. A pink salmon was set out below; white potatoes sprinkled with parsley lay revealed on lifting another. He began to eat with relish.

He knew that he was not in sufficient touch with what was out there, beyond the circuit of the chauffeured car, the committee room, the briefing session by the young civil servants, Oxford people like himself. But there was no way now to get in touch. He was undermined by his own privilege - the upbringing in the country house in Gloucestershire, his father the circuit judge. There had been Eton, Oxford, his own flat provided also in Kensington. In his case the clichés were all true. He had never lacked anything. He knew how those in opposition regarded him. Yet it hadn't been his fault to be born as he had been. He felt depressed, as if the privileges were a trick practised on him. When it had all been secure, he never reflected in this way. Perhaps he must trim his sails to continue to rise. An irritable ambition never left him. He must get up. He would go to see elsewhere.

The bell rang in the secretary's office. "The car, please. I'm going to those East suburbs."

"Certainly, Sir." For him it had always been certainly. Discreetly the secret police set off in front of his white car, with a tail also behind. He knew that this way he could never experience life down there. A huge gap had existed since his silvery birth between himself, his type, and the rest. It hadn't been his fault. But should such a person have governmental power? He felt slightly sick, to be out, unaccustomed. He would like to go out, later, shooting down the low in revenge for the insecurities they made him feel. Now he recalled adages of the previous Prime Minister, how the present one felt the same: 'the public is an idiot who tends to believe in us as authorities to respect. We can do anything.' Yet the riots were well organised, dislike in some zones was becoming widespread, active. What could be done? Why should his own sort be inconvenienced?

The car moved anonymous along the dual carriageway packed with vehicles. Tall blocks rose up on each side, ugly and blank. The Chancellor had joked with him - 'Most people don't have a clue what goes on, they've no idea of the stock exchange, banking, business, nothing. We can do what we like, so long', and here the Chancellor had grown earnest, 'so long as we keep the money people with us.' He, a junior minister then, had nodded deferential agreement. Intoxicated with his recent promotion he'd taken in the smiles of power, wanted to reach the upper point. Now he was there. Only lately it had started to go wrong, uneasy feelings had come.

A traffic light blocked the way. He peered out, aimless. An orange sign over a drab building proclaimed Job Centre. Usually he paid no attention to the outer environment, busy with papers. The outside other people lived in was different to his own. A weird queue of people lined the pavement, black men with ringleted hair, pale, dingy, white men, punks, girls in plastic skirts. Who were they? He'd never known anyone who was anything like one of these. How could he grasp what £25 a week meant? One of the youths gave him the V sign as he stared from the big car, mouthed something. The chauffeur glanced back. "Disgusting, Sir, how some of them are. No education. It's these teachers, all gays and left wingers." The minister was annoyed, his remoteness disturbed, and merely glanced coldly at the driver.

This was now the riot area. The council estate stretched for miles, unrelieved. Cars without wheels, headlamps, were dumped in lay-bys outside houses; youths and girls looked jeeringly as the big cars passed. But in the jeer was also envy, the desire to make it, to be rich, at the top with the power to buy and buy. Few people were about. Shop windows were meshed to prevent break-ins, smash and grab raids. An atmosphere of dirty futility hung over the zone: here the low lived. It was the opposite to the Cirencester the minister knew, the polo park and country house. He was uneasy. How had such a place grown up to start with? Who had planned it? Something out of control was imminent, because thought had been lost too far back, the meaning had gone.

The secret service men were pulling into a lay-by, indicating he too should stop. They stood around, men in grey suits, expensive like stockbrokers, but guns in the pockets here in the English suburb, guards of the establishment. This was their job, to protect those who had power regardless. They liked to serve the right. The civil servant also got out of the vehicle, behind. He had an eager white face, black glasses, feeble limbs, had also been to Oxford. The droney voice of the superior class started jarringly up. "You see, Sir, conditions aren't good in the houses. There's damp, the rents are high. And in this area, jobs are scarce. Most are on benefits of some kind. They've got nothing."

"They deserve it, though, don't they?"

"Yes. As you are well aware, the Prime Minister is strongly against propping up unprofitable units; if conditions are improved, incentive for self-betterment recedes."

The minister nodded. This was true. People should help themselves. A group of youths began to gather on the pavement opposite the cars. The men in power ignored them, got back into the vehicles. Enough time had been spent seeing, and the meeting with the police was waiting.

The youths were in the class. Sixteen, seventeen, they'd had to come back to school because there were no jobs. The dusty classroom was somewhere to go, warmer than the street, when the heating worked. They weren't eligible for the dole as they could be 'trained', the government said, half days at the school, half days as garage or shop helps. It was unpaid labour, and no training took place. They were up, eyes sharp, for the fight. "Wanker!" The cry rose up as the teacher entered. They wanted easy trouble to escape their own minimal lives.

Back on the bus some swung vicious from the luggage inset rails, shouting abuse, obscenities. The traffic packed along the dusty main road between the council houses. They saw the white car pass in a blur, the fattish, white-faced small man in the back. A jeer went up that was also envy. He'd got on, to be up there. They too would like to be ministers, on top, full of power. Some respected these upper men, like members of a privileged Reich, as did many other English. Some wanted greater strictness, would have liked smart uniforms for the leaders, rallies and military displays.

The estate was quiet. Heaps of rubbish lay on the grass. Groups of youths stood in entries. A sniggering started up: "Can't get in again, Gary? Your mum's out again. With her nigger!" A great chant of derision went up, a teenage boy looked uncomfortable. All enjoyed his misery as it meant their own, often similar, would be overlooked this time.

Older men stood at a distance, watching. One scrambled down to the entrance area from the dirty raised lawn, sidestepping overturned supermarket trolleys abandoned on

the concrete courtyard, approached a group that had separated from the rest. The youths here, and a large group of
unemployed men, turned to him with respect.

"Tonight, then. It's on." The group nodded, collectively
sharp now, the desultory, lost mood gone. "Same place.
See you." The man was gone again, back up the bank,
passing on elsewhere.

The police were getting ready. The vans with meshed
windows, reinforced bodies, were being loaded. Police with
new riot shields were climbing on board. There were jokes,
"Kill them, toast them in ovens like that dog they cooked."
Recently a popular newspaper run by a millionaire had
featured the baking of a dog by teenagers as a headline.
But some younger constables, were uneasy. They themselves had come from the estate, didn't like civil war.

The minister had spoken to them all, that afternoon.
Ushered in to the assembly room at police headquarters,
flanked as always by his bodyguards, he had represented
actual power. A flutter of respect had gone up from the
policemen, at the sight. He had made it, he was also on
their side. He was their aspiration.

"You see, men," and here the minister had eyed them
lingeringly, emphasising he was a man like them, shared a
life like theirs, "the Prime Minister is especially anxious
that an example should be made tonight. The riots have
been getting worse: tonight you must show who is in charge.
I know you can do your best. I know you are with us.
Remember, these people are nothing: unemployed men,
the poor, immigrants, youths. They are riff-raff to be subdued." He passed an easy hand over his grey hair, elegant,
spoke delicately. "Use all the legal means you have." He
winked, man to man. "Whatever you do, we're with you."
He turned, walked briskly to the door, flanked by the se-
vere guards. A buzz of excitement went round the officers.
"Bastards, we'll get them. They're just reds, niggers, teenies.
Let's get them." The men were pent up, ready.

Darkness was falling. The vans ran in convoy along the

149

drab high street of the suburb. All was familiar, the usual, ugly, cheap shops, supermarkets, furniture and video stores, tasteless modern structures. Some shops had signs saying claimants of benefit could obtain discounts. Business was so bad, even the poorest were welcome, had to be wooed to buy. An underpass loomed up ahead. The vans were through, emerging onto the motorway, speeding east, confident.

The men were walking, smashing windows of banks, big stores, kicking in the headlamps of the larger cars and gouging scratches down the sides. The vans were approaching. They started to run, towards the tower blocks. Four stood up nearby like concrete keeps, linked by aerial walkways. The police were running now, the boots heavy, sinister on the concrete paths. Suddenly, from an underground car park came a group of a hundred people, emerging quickly out of the darkness. The bottles they held were alight, white fuses burned; thrown, they exploded in blasts of glass and fire. A line of burning separated the rioters and the police. The police stopped, as did the men. There was a tension and silence in the night. Other residents on the estate were invisible, locked in their rooms, or else lurking at the rear of the younger men. Some older people had also emerged; poorly paid men, unemployed, people with little to lose and filled with backlogs of hate, violence, vistas, until now, of their own powerlessness.

The car swung home, off the motorway. The minister headed for Hertfordshire. In the spring evening light the fields spread out, as the London suburbs were left behind. Other successful men, managers, directors, bankers, brokers, were also returning to their large houses beyond St. Albans. There was a shared world of assumptions, comfort to come, the pleasures cash success had brought. The minister was anxious to get home, to be met at the oak panelled door by his wife. He eyed the chauffeur, saw the thin, slightly greasy black hair combed to the respectable two inches above the collar. Although this man was one of his supporters he felt a repulsion for his nasty lowness, his greasy, furtive aspect. A queer curiosity filled him. He rapped sharply on the glass. "Jack - what will you do tonight?"

The driver eyed the fattish man in the mirror. "I'll have eats, Sir, then watch T.V. It's Eastenders. Then there'll be a video, Emmanuelle Four. Then bed, I might read some of that thriller book your colleague wrote, if I can't get off."

"How are your children?"

"Two just got some C.S.E.s. Very low grades, I'm afraid. They're leaving school, job-hunting, Sir."

The minister reflected, without reply. This man had his own life, down there, his own council house, amusements, children. He read books. So how could there be discontent? There must be millions similar, ready to respect and buy. How was he any different to his chauffeur in tastes and aspirations, except in the amount of cash he had at his own disposal? All was well in England. But a dark awareness came again. He didn't know what it was, this other world, glimpsed that morning, of the ugly council houses, the poor. He disliked it for being ugly, cashlessly aping back at him his own vulgarity and implication.

The car turned left into a leafy road, then ran up a red gravelled driveway, through black wrought iron gates. Expensive antique lamps from coaching days stuck out of the house wall on each side of the front door. The house was large, mock Georgian. Inside it would be comfortable. The queer feeling came to him; he was in the right world. Others were negligibles. He repressed the desire to speak obscenities to Jack, give him a lash across his ugly neck. In the past coachmen had been whipped. He wanted violence, against the low who threatened his aplomb.

Inside, his wife came to greet him. She was about fifty years old, but looked younger. Like him, she had never been down. Part of her fancy, though, was that she constituted a more liberal, imaginative half of the relation, to complement her husband's ruthless effectiveness in the outer

world. A few books even lay in her bedroom; on the dressing table, also among the frilly curtains that hung below,
were banal volumes by Iris Murdoch, even Martin Amis -
innocuous, untaxing works that could be passed off, though,
as modern, intelligent, in bourgeois conversation. She had
the reputation of being cultured in the circles she moved
in. "Darling, the riots. They're on television now. Those
ungrateful people! But the police are doing a wonderful
job."

He moved quickly, in charge, across the deeply carpeted
room, past the floral material of the settee, until the set
was in view. There, in colour, were the blocks, the line of
fire, the police crouching behind shields, the rioters a distant blur of huddled shapes. A commentator was reassuring, explaining. It was darker now; the red fires lit up
misshaped heaps of rubbish on the black lawns. One of the
blocks itself was on fire. A few placards were propped up
with amateurish captions: 'We've got no jobs our homes
are damp.' The minister was pleased to see these. He knew
how in general such claims met with little sympathy among
most English people. When the low protest it isn't serious.
On the other hand, it is serious when financial managers
or company directors inform audiences of lazy workers,
slackers, when ministers explain the essential, overriding
need for a competitive, materialist, social view. A smile
crossed his face. The police had a new weapon to use later.
He imagined the surprise of the rioters.

But he was also divided. Part of him would have liked
to go with the rioters, jeering at the police, spitting on
them, defiling that which he most explicitly endorsed. A
secret attraction to low class women also titillated him -
he'd seen them, that afternoon, some in cheap plastic looking high heeled shoes, tarty slit skirts. He could go with
one, just to look. This secret name for such women,
'prosties', swelled up in his mind, exciting him. A porno-
graphic sub-text ran; one could even piss on him, rope him
up. Or he could sit in a wheel chair, watch one undress.

For money they'd do anything, these people.

The news changed; in Japan a dog had swum two miles across an estuary to reach its master, the Queen had looked slightly tired at church. Nothing would be attended to. All was right in the world. So it would seem to the majority he knew. He recalled the words of the Home Secretary, consoling: 'The people are sluggish, stupid. Short of absolute disaster they can't identify sickness. They will never know what we really are, see us in our indifference up at our own level.' It was true; his own world, Hertfordshire, the London club, polo at Cirencester - no-one came there but men and women like himself. England was a network of worlds, all simultaneous, but sealed off each from each, inaccessible. In their council houses people existed merely moronic, he knew, with their trivial papers and the excitement of television and videos, materialist fantasies. He himself mixed with the millionaires who owned these papers, made the videos, employed the low. Money cast a plausible gloss over the blankness of the upper levels. Money gained respect and obedience. Aspirations were much the same, upper and lower, but there was no mixing.

A queer whim came. He would go himself to the riot zone, be seen with the police. He went upstairs, got down an old mac, gardening trousers. He could remove this disguise when he was past the rioters. Unfit, he panted slightly as he climbed the stairs. His wife was used to his sudden disappearance on business, made no protest.

The car swept towards the poor suburbs, where the simple lived. He was excited, seeing the police lights ahead. Now two of the blocks seemed to be alight and the fire brigade watched helpless, unable to get near. From the blocks he could hear with vague surprise the tense crack of gunfire. Was it the police? Or was it a new development in civil disobedience? He drew closer, showed a pass to the officer at the cordon that marked the forbidden area.

"The other ministers are here too, Sir." The officer gestured towards an armoured vehicle nearby, big like a luxury

153

committee room inside. To be on the scene could help promotion. Inside a tall, gaunt man with a long head and body like a mute's at a Victorian funeral was pacing, while a crippled woman in a wheelchair watched, her face white and sharp. "They're bastards, these subversive types. Failures of evolution!" The mute was elegant in his expensive suit, with red veins in the blue eyes giving a strained, fanatic look. He spoke in the drawling accent of the always privileged. "They're like the ones who tried to bomb me." His tone was outraged; it didn't occur to him that he was a legitimate target. The crippled woman, his wife and secretary, began to froth and mutter. "The police should be strong, strong, strong. The Prime Minister said they should. You should give them the instruction now." Her chair rocked and twitched as she jerked there, anxious to be at them.

The man's eyes were bloodshot; his thin body looked frail, his long fingers vicious. The other minister was put in sudden mind of a teacher he'd had at Eton who'd had similar hands. The master would creep up behind the recalcitrant, poke him in the spine, wrap his umbrella handle round the neck and tug it. Or else he'd invite other boys to slap the malefactor down. "They should be slapped down - the complainers." The minister spun round, guilty; had his thoughts been read? The crippled woman was still on: "The P.M. says we should slap them down. All who aren't belongers." The mute nodded in grave agreement.

The pair were left in the armoured room, portable to trouble zones. The minister left them alone with their task, to liaise with the Prime Minister by radio-telephone. It seemed that night the P.M. had chosen to take a personal interest in the affair. Outside it was quiet. He walked between the rows of waiting police. They were drawn up, a reserve force, a mile from the burning blocks. It made them feel important to see the high official walking there, in their midst.

Suddenly a great shout went up, in the distance, and a

huge light flared in the sky. There was a sound of explosion, detonated material. The reserve force moved forward. The minster ran with them, in the excitement. A heap of blue uniforms lay ahead, confused, bleeding. "They had bazookas," - he registered distantly the shouts of explanation. He saw the wide muzzle swing at the balcony half way up a block; other muzzles also loomed. He must be in their sights. Shambling behind he saw also the mute, jolting madly the woman in the wheelchair over the stony grass, running at random. He raised his hand to wave them back. Then he knew from the whining darkness he was as well the target; the missile sought out him, the vans behind, the army units that were assembling. A wheel of the chair rose up, grotesque in the flare of the army search lights; he watched the mute blow away, his own hand lie on the lawn by a heap of old crisp packets, the blood flow down onto the jumble of rubbish. Then he was gone.

The Prime Minister was in the office, alone. The news was bad. Across the night she could see the flares of separate fires, hear the shooting even near her. There was a rattle at the window, the quick sound of a security lock unfixing. A grotesque grey head, encased in an elegant woman's Fogal stocking, peered at her. The minister saw the gun raised, registered the light pap as the bullet hit. The new time was coming. As she fell, the magazine slipped from her fingers, laid open. The article was on power dressing, and showed a series of wealthy men, immaculate, except for limp penises hanging loose, exposed. The minister's own skirt had been dishevelled as the window had opened. Her opponent gave the dead hand a quick sniff, recoiled in disgust at the acrid odour, and kicked the body aside in some amusement. Filths savour but themselves; this line came to the young girl's head. It had been true, of this upper group, in any case.

THE CARPET SELLER

The man was standing in front of the mirror, adjusting his tie. The mirror had a gold, ornate frame. On the floor lay a darkly patterned Persian carpet. He turned to go back to his bedroom. A half open door revealed a flourish of pink bed-spreads and pink wall-paper; another dark blue Persian carpet lay in there. In the daytime the river was visible from the big window, through branches of tall trees.. On the far side were the docks. Now it was night time and the snow was falling.

The man went on, into the bedroom, where his wife was dressing. He was tall and spare, about fifty years old. In his face was a curious, dissolute look, at odd variance with the general impression of goodwill he tried to give. He moved oddly, his feet stuck out at a sharp angle from his legs; his stomach was swollen, like a pregnant woman's. Even so, there was a certain sleek boniness about him. Now, putting on his black overcoat, he looked the business success he really was. The man's dark Persian features went with acquired European manners and habits of dress. He had lived here, in Hamburg for the last fifteen years. The carpet import business was good. He smoked a pipe, prosperous and genial. But in his eyes was a defeat of some kind.

His wife was twenty-five years younger than he was. He had been married twice before. The new wife had been with him for two years. He had pursued her heavily, given her plane tickets back to Teheran when she was studying in Germany, tried to make her indebted to him. He had gone to the places where he knew she would be. In the end he had gone to Teheran, asked the girl's father if the daughter would marry him. The father had been pleased at the idea of connection with so important a businessman. The girl acquiesced in the male desires that surrounded her.

Now the husband spoke jokingly to his wife, in Persian. She replied sharply, almost mocking. But at the same time, she was under his control. By instinct she felt the man was her master, even if she didn't like him. She looked up at her husband from her large eyes. She seemed weary, almost ill. Yet her luxurious form, voluptuous, had a passive

159

vitality, independent of her circumstance. Now she was choosing what to wear. The wardrobe door was open wide; expensive skirts and dresses hung from racks inside. She could console herself with these.

A guest was waiting in the drawing room. On a long table, in front of an elegant sofa with silk braid hanging from its longest edge, stood a large bowl of fruit, plates of nuts, sweets. The Persians were warm and lavish in their hospitality. The television was on but no-one was watching it. The Persian wife liked to hear it in the background, even in the daytime. Then, when everyone was out, except for this visitor and herself, she would get up late, clean the flat, switch on the television, phone her friends with the set audible in the background. She was afraid to be by herself with nothing to do. In the afternoons she would often go shopping for clothes, in the centre of the German town, to distract herself. But she was dissatisfied with her life, almost in despair, beneath the surface composure and habits.

The flat was lively now, with the preparations. They were all going out. In the day time it was sometimes dreary, in spite of the luxury. The woman was lost in the vacant perfection of it all. Yet it gratified her to live in these surroundings. She would find it hard to live with less. At the back of the flat, some distance below, the Elbe flowed sullen and grey. The diseased water rocked up against the concrete banks on each side as the ships passed. In daylight you could see the big ships, moving slowly, while tall cranes swung in the yards opposite. The flat itself though, was insulated, quite cut off from the outside activity.

The woman was unaware of the depth of her discontent. Only she sensed a vacancy in herself, like a distant illness. "I want to leave my husband," she had told her visitor often. As she spoke, the visitor realised she didn't believe she could leave; her dark eyes, though wide open, were veiled with unexpressed despair. "It was my father - he said, marry this man. I was young, I thought he knew

160

best." She looked to her guest, to interpret her experience. She had met him in England, invited him to Germany. Her husband hadn't objected. "He has many girlfriends while I'm away. Don't you?" she would turn to her husband, jeering in part, because she couldn't be enough for him. He smiled back, weary. "Yes, of course, I am a man. I cannot live without a woman."

Now the girl came forward, into the sitting room. She was wearing golden shoes that lifted her heels high off the ground, and a thin black smock over black silk trousers. Gold bracelets hung round her wrists. The old Persian desire for sensuous splendour still worked in her. Only her eyes looked tired and ill. The voluptuous weight of her form seemed separate from her life here, not implicated. She looked almost larger than life. She had given herself up to this wealthy world and it was now her enclosure. But her nature and upbringing was also of this world; without money and luxury she would suffer.

The husband was ready. He came out through the hallway, treading lightly on the Persian carpet with its rich colours glowing in the soft light. She looked at him mockingly again, but in appraisal. Although she didn't love him, she wanted him to look well beside her. With her husband she completed a picture of wealth and success. But in the background, in the woman, was an uncertainty, a shadow of something shut back and stifled. However, she also loved her glory.

"You know - I must have a woman. When my wife is not here, I must have someone." The husband spoke up to his guest as they were leaving. "In London there are very nice girls." he continued, about to start an anecdote of his past experience. "Yes, he has many girlfriends - all different nationalities" interrupted his wife. She was teasing him. The older man was pleased at the mockery. His eyes were old, withdrawn, as if he could no longer see anything clearly. He was non-existent to himself, except as the recipient of sensations. His body looked peculiar, with the

161

fat, bulging stomach belying the trimness elsewhere. "To-night we go to a sex-show. You like?"

Together they clattered down the concrete staircase beyond the front door of the apartment. Outside it was freezing, with snow falling in thick heavy flakes. It was pleasant to be out of the heavy heat of indoors. The young woman got into the front seat of the long white car. She took for granted this affluent life. She was wearing a black fur coat that matched her dark black hair. It was obvious she knew her husband's requirements and how to handle him. She handed him his pipe, with silent mockery. The car set off along the wide road, with big houses in spacious gardens on each side. It was the most exclusive part of the city. The guest sat quietly in the back of the car. "Say something, then. You are too silent." The girl turned to him, smiling. She liked her visitor. It was the first time she had had a friend to stay. He was young and could talk to her about her emotions. He seemed to understand her, she felt. Only she didn't like it when he went absent, wrapped himself about in his own thoughts. The husband began to talk, smoking his pipe, with Persian music playing in the background.

He turned to the Englishman. "You know, you aren't happy. You are always alone. You must laugh, enjoy yourself." The girl joined in: "You should have many girlfriends, make love to them." The man smiled - he enjoyed their mock concern. Life to these Persians was a pleasure, a gift, fascinating. But life was equated with pleasure absolutely. Anything that couldn't be categorized as pleasant was excluded. As a result more difficult activities were left out. Justice, empathy, thought, imagination were in general too troublesome. Each individual's task was to maximise his own pleasure. The husband was rooted in this credo. His wife was vaguely conscious that it didn't answer every situation. The guest had no belief in it - he was watchful, he wanted to see what was involved.

Sex was one of the pleasures. It hurt the Persian to see

162

this young man so restrained. "The more women I have, the happier I am." The older man announced this, as a fact. Yet his eyes still showed a trouble and dissatisfaction. There was a puzzling honesty about his inclinations, which went with a failure to criticize or consider them.

The car ran along the avenue of the suburb. On one side tall trees stood in a deserted park, weighed down by snow. There was a curious, empty atmosphere - no-one walked on the pavements. Inside the car it was warm, cut off from outside influence. They drove on, not talking. Suddenly they swung off the main road onto a side street. In spite of the icy cold, girls stood along the pavement, in doorways. The wife watched them whimsically out of the window. A man always wanted a woman. She was amused, accepting. She felt she was in the camp of those who were desired. At the same time she was furtive about her interest.

"Come, let's walk." They stepped out onto the frozen street. The Persian walked forward, urbane in his black coat. What was it that impelled him so often to this area? There was a lurid fascination in him for this suburb devoted to prostitutes and sex shows. The wife and guest followed his eager figure, stepping out on the icy pavement. "See those cars?" The man turned to the pair behind. "They belong to the pimps." He pointed to a row of big black cars lined up along the kerb. The guest wasn't sure what to expect. He couldn't understand the excitement of his hosts. The woman's reaction was like her husband's, only more concealed. She was intrigued, almost fascinated. The prostitutes cast worn looks at each passer by. Some couldn't have been older than fourteen.

They passed into an arcade which led to a dark public precinct. "I will show you something, come." The older man led the guest along the dark passage. There in the precinct stood a crowd of women dressed only in underclothes and boots. Some wore fur coats loosely draped around them. Men stood and watched. The Persian walked about, in control of the situation, pointing out the women he preferred. He felt himself master of the pleasures these women might provide.

The three of them turned back and entered a club that stood opposite the precinct entrance. They sat at dark tables drinking whisky. The room was small and the velvet seats were red and shabby. The wife sat between the two men, smiling faintly. She knew what men wanted, she felt. She touched the guest lightly with her knee under the table. He responded to her. He was watching the stage. Why shouldn't a woman dance naked if she chose? At this time, there seemed no reason. If there was a reason he didn't care about it. The curtains of the small stage stayed pulled. The audience was also small; a few business men and a group of tired Japanese students sat in the darkness on rows of tiered seats. At the back of the hall a group of girls stood, dressed briefly in glimmering dresses. The place was amateurish, almost good-humoured. The curtains were drawn open.

A woman walked onto the stage in front of a roughly painted piece of scenery. She was at the station. Her husband, a ridiculous tall German in shorts, was saying goodbye to her. A porter appeared with a trolley, and stood in the background. Electric music played. The Persian woman smiled at her husband and guest. The porter ran his hand across the woman's thigh, below her skirt, pulled her blouse open to reveal her breasts. She undid his trousers. They made love as she lay back on the luggage trolley. The audience watched amused, even intrigued; yes, such a situation was possible, why not represent it? In a sense it was a true representation: such a woman might want to act like that. Why not? The scene ended and the audience clapped. It was a little like an amateur production in an English church hall - an atmosphere of benevolent tolerance seemed to prevail in the audience, good-will. The audience settled back in good humour to wait for the next turn. Meanwhile the woman and the man who had just appeared came out and sat at the back of the hall.

The Persian husband was intrigued by the act. "Did you notice, how long he went on? Two hundred times! Could you go on so long?" He asked the question almost naively wanting to know the answer. "Maybe," the guest replied. He hadn't really considered the issue. "Quite a while, anyway, I suppose." The husband seemed to be considering the information. His wife joined in. "We brought my sister and my old auntie here last time." It was true. The old Persian woman had sat back and enjoyed the show, laughing out loud at some of the turns, and considering it a normal European entertainment. "My sister - she couldn't believe the size of the black man's penis. 'Was it real', she asked me." The girl went off into a ring of laughter at the recollection. The guest was mildly amused. What world was this?

The curtains opened again. The loudspeakers played a complicated abstract piece of German electronic music. Slides of cosmic scenes, planetary landscapes, even Blake pictures, were shone onto a screen in the centre of the stage, across the walls. Behind a thin gauze curtain knelt two naked girls. In the centre of the curtain in front, was a throne. The music mounted to a peak of sound as the king moved off the throne to initiate the women into his service. Each one had to be made love to on a couch in front of the gauze curtain.

The scenes passed; the audience relaxed more and more. More whisky was bought. The Persian wife sat easily in her chair. Her husband watched the acts with an air of urbane evaluation, praising particular attributes of the women, costumes that pleased him, or details of the dramatic action he especially admired. The guest was interested in the show, taking his own pleasure in the nakedness of the women and the excess of their costumes.

It was time to leave; the show was over. The audience filed out, good humoured. Some of the men would go on to other shows, or perhaps return to the precinct to hire one of the girls there for a few hours. The Persian girl went off

165

to the ladies room. Her husband drew the guest aside. He liked to confide in him. "You know, in London too there are many girls from Iran. They all like sex. They can't stop, once they start. The develop a taste for it. I was in the Playboy club - I saw a friend. He said, downstairs, in my ear, I have two girls. Come with me. So all night long, making love, laughing. Next time I'll call you." He spoke in broken English, anxious to offer a pleasure. The guest watched his host's eyes; they were dark, veiled with a suggestion of defeat. A man liked women; well then, why shouldn't he enjoy them, if they didn't mind? There was no reason. The guest grinned, clapped the other man across the shoulders. But for himself he doubted that an endless succession of encounters would be satisfying.

The girl came towards the men, smiling, with the black fur collar of her coat turned up. Next to her husband she looked warm, slightly mischievous. A vivid light shone in her brown eyes. "Yes, you must have more women. What is wrong with you?" She turned, joking, to the visitor. She seemed immune, to him, in a world of money, expensive restaurants, plane tickets, wardrobes of expensive clothes. But she had another, fresher self that wanted expression. She took hold of the guest's arm. She was half-pleased, half-puzzled by his restraint. On the surface, her husband didn't mind what she did.

The large white car was warm; they moved fast along the wide road, with the lights of the docks flashing beside them. They were quickly away, separated from the world they had just been in. The car, the trappings, all belonged to another sphere of money and pleasing yourself; like the flat these things belonged to one who controlled his own workforce and set down his own conditions. It was easy to be casual, irresponsible, behind the barrier of such material goods and potentials. It was the modern myth made actual: rise up, get the money, enjoy yourself.

In the daytime the Persian ran his carpet business; the rest of his time was the pursuit of pleasure. But did he find it finally? The guest glanced at his face as he drove; his eyes sagged in the lined flesh, still hungry. The woman was no fool; she knew she could not find what she wanted in such a life. Only she could not make conscious for herself what was missing. So she tried to involve herself in the pleasure pursuit, dressing up finely, shopping, going out to restaurants and clubs with her husband and his friends. Her own unexpressed sexuality was a heavy burden within her. She couldn't relate to her husband, except just in submission. Her own richness was turning to inertia and nervousness. They swung into the driveway.

Outside the snow was freezing hard; it broke crisply as they walked towards the house. The air was sharp and cold; trees stuck up vaguely into the darkness. This outside world was vigorous and fresh, alert. Inside they sat on the expensive settees, arranged at right angles, at the end of the long half-lit lounge. The room was beautiful, with tall green plants at one side, lit up gently by table lamps. In each room lay a Persian carpet. The girl looked across at the guest, quizzically, smiling again. Her husband brought out a bottle of brandy. There was an odd, relaxed bond between them all. The woman curled up in her chair, cheerful. The husband got up: "I'm going to bed: enjoy yourselves." It was curious, how easily he left his wife with the other man. Could he really be so indifferent? It was mysterious.

Before the guest had arrived, she had told her husband the younger man was her lover; the husband had acquiesced in this. There was a curious detachment about him. He had a final indifference to anything beyond the momentary; only in business could he persist beyond the moment. "I enjoy myself," was his favourite self-explanation. His wife felt cheated and left out by such a philosophy. She had never loved the older man in any case. She had believed all girls should act as she had. After all, marriage was more an arrangement for her comfort and security than an issue of deeper relating. This was her parents' creed. Now she wanted a real friend, who she could trust. She wanted to love someone.

The girl moved, now her husband was gone, to sit beside her visitor. She loved to tease him. "Well . . . do you still want me?" She opened her large dark eyes, wide, and gazed at him. It was a sort of game for her, but also she really wanted the man. He was aware of her warm presence beside him, with a sudden surprise and relief. She touched his arm. "Come, let's go to your room." She went in front of him across the hall-way, gently lit by a small lamp, to a square room with a Chinese carpet on the floor. The carpet glowed a rich blue; a strange looking bird struggled on it to raise itself, within white borders. Another small light cast a glow in the room. In the daytime there was an atmosphere of sterility about the flat, of wasted energy and money, without vivid life. But now this small room was also beautiful. She kissed him briefly. "Go to sleep," she told him, quickly, "I will come back."

He undressed slowly and lay on the white mattress set out on the floor, Persian style. He turned off the light. Cars ran past on the road below the window, muffled in the snow. He lay there for some minutes, until the door clicked open. "Don't move! Did I surprise you?" She was laughing. She pulled out another mattress from a cupboard and spread it next to his. She was wearing a white nightdress that fitted her quite tightly; her heavy breasts hung forward loosely as she bent over her work. He touched her, sure of his desire for her. She was always laughing and joking. Her rich form seemed made for sensuality.

"Well?" She looked at him again, always laughing. "How are your girlfriends?" The room was dark. By a chink of light between the blue velvet curtains, he saw her face looking at him. He didn't find her face beautiful but responded to a warm glow she seemed to contain and send out to touch him. He liked her teasing very much. He reached out to run his hand along her arm. She smiled again and moved closer, pressing his other hand across her breasts. She turned to him, moving so she was accessible. This was a new, moist reality, a rich centre for them both. There was an infinite unlimited aspect to it all that surprised the man.

It was strange how her husband didn't seem to mind. "Did you enjoy yourself - last night?" he asked them both at breakfast. They all sat round a small table in the kitchen by the window overlooking the river. Outside the trees were weighed down with snow. The girl wore a loose black dressing-gown, made of silk, tied casually. She smiled at the question. But also she looked ill, with heavy eyes. She didn't want to figure in her husband's imagination. "I am so worried - why did I marry him? What can I do?" She had often repeated this to her guest. She was thinking it again now. A strange smile was in the husband's face. "I'm going to work. You two stay here." The smile was almost kind, with a weariness in it that came from following sensation to sensation; nothing really mattered to him. The others were behind him in sensational understanding. So, in a way, he saw them as his children. He wanted to be a sensational guide, a provider.

The door shut behind him. The woman sat at the table, with a small glass of Persian tea in front of her. She watched the man appraisingly and with pleasure, touching his hair. "You know - when it was my wedding - I didn't feel it was me, who was getting married. I enjoyed the party, and tried to ignore him. Afterwards he wanted to sleep with me. But I wouldn't let him . . ." She trailed off and looked out of the window. "So, I was stupid to marry him." She laughed again. The visitor listened, feeling a warm sympathy and liking for her. "Why did you marry him at all?"

"I was young, my father said do that. He seemed to want me. Now my father shrugs his shoulders when I tell him I'm miserable. I suppose life is like this."

She went to the sitting room and pulled out a photograph album of the wedding from a drawer. The Persian women took such things very seriously. One of the girl's

169

friends had had a film made of her own, for example. There stood the bride in a long white dress surrounded by fussing, elegant female relatives, in jewels and expensive clothes. In another picture she was by her husband who wore a black suit. It was all a scene of wealth, but there was also a liveliness that wasn't English, an atmosphere as well of warmth and enjoyment. She had liked the party, being the centre of attention. She hadn't really considered her feeling for her husband - he was an adjunct, a provider of the show. She had supposed that every girl should have a husband, and that in the absence of much personal feeling any girl would sensibly choose one who could provide her with most things, a luxurious home, clothes, a social position. This was what she had done. Before the ceremony costly gifts had come down on her; this was the custom and each woman expected these at her wedding as her due. There were the diamond necklace from the husband's parents, earrings, other rings for her hands, clothes. It was a show of wealth, conventional.

She went to put the book away. She got up to get dressed, kissing the man lightly as she passed. "Come to help me." She liked to show herself to the man, make love to him. They spent many days like this, in the flat, talking, making love, until the husband returned.

Sometimes there were visitors. It was the weekend and the three of them were expecting another Iranian, just arrived in Germany. The rich man came forward, carrying a mixture of bags. In his right hand was an expensive modern suitcase. In his left was a carrier bag, prominently labelled with a famous designer's name. He offered it to the Persian wife.

He was short, immaculately dressed, ridiculous. He settled down on the settee, importantly. The wife took off her package and peeped inside. It was an expensive scarf. "Thank you." She talked only briefly, went off to her room.

It was small this world, and tight. The luxurious flat, the visitors, the trips to the shops, the restaurants, this was all. The guest could enjoy it, as a sensual pleasure. But in the end these things led nowhere, petered out.

He was caught in a sensual underworld with the woman. As she came back into the room, wearing a thin silk dress, he could only appreciate her. She smiled, seeing him look at her. The other men were talking business at the far end of the room. "You know - it's much better with you. The others - they talk of selling. But I like to talk to you." She sat down next to him. "Teach me some English." She really wanted to learn. She liked also to be caught up in a special world with the man, to be just with him. There was a desire in her to live that wouldn't find expression in this rich world. Even so, she was bound in to it.

The new visitor had found a copy of Playboy in a pile of books under the table. The Englishman knew that in a cupboard of the oak-style wall unit was kept a little stack of sex magazines. The husband liked to read these. They dealt with brief narratives with photographs to match - 'Tara from the office invited me home to tea. I little expected when I rang the bell to be welcomed by . . .' and so the narratives continued. The new guest began an anecdote. "At Frankfurt - I was alone. So I rang through for an escort. She was a good, big girl." The two Persians discussed the episode, like epicurean sages, conferring in judgment. The room with all its weight of material wealth gave the discussion a sanction it would have lacked, had it taken place in a slum-room. These were rich, successful men who had earned their pleasures. But did it matter - the magazines, the episodes, the clubs - who cared? Was it any worse than the dreary virtue of work and its morality? At least here the people acted, instead of fantasising.

But the enjoyment was momentary - it led just to the desire for more, on and on, uncounted. The girl took no part in these discussions about sexual adventures. Only she was interested to know how her own sex could be considered by men. Was this all they wanted? Her husband's view of life as pleasure, of women, influenced her view of herself. Only there was a real kindness in her that prevented her going so far as him. She could not just be immune, a queen unto herself, only considering what she wanted, and disregarding the rest. She had too instinctive a sense of others as existing in their own right to be purely consuming. She liked her guest, sensually and as a friend. As for him, he gravitated towards her warm, full body and laughing nature like a man who moves towards what he needs.

Outside it was growing dark. "We must go out - to the warehouse." The husband vanished to fetch his coat. The new visitor had been talking in French to the English guest. He had once been cultural attaché to the Iran Embassy in Paris and worked there still as a diplomat. While he spoke, the Englishman watched the other's neat, handmade grey shoes, took in the sharp crease in the cream trousers, the thin belt, the tailored cream jacket. This was all part of the reward for serving the Shah. Plainly the diplomat saw no contradiction between the Persian culture he 'represented' and his present position. He was urbane, a success. Those opposed to the Shah might be arrested, tortured, but meanwhile he was secure and affluent. "These troubles in Teheran - they are terrible." But if it was obvious the Shah would be defeated he would switch his allegiances to the successor.

The diplomat was aware that when he was out with the husband, the English guest would be alone with the wife - his manner conveyed that he understood this arrangement. The Englishman liked to be incorporated in the unspoken acknowledgement. At least he was being treated as a man, with desires. In England desires were in general taboo.

The girl got up to draw the curtains, There was a warm, sensual atmosphere in the room. He got up to look out of the big window, through the gap between the two velvet curtains. There were the lights of the big ships moving downstream with the tide, full of German goods. He could hear the soft churning of the propellers as the boats passed.

172

THE CARPET SELLER

It was quiet, so high up, looking down over the wharves to the wide stretch of industrial river, just visible. The room seemed to have no relation with the world down below. It was a rich retreat. The woman had disappeared to the bedroom. He heard her call him. It was what he wanted - to sink down with her into a world of warmth and pleasure, to feel the shocks of passion shake him and her. They didn't think about it. It was natural, unencumbered. He liked that too, the simplicity. There was no protestation of love, nothing said, just an exchange of warmth and softness, in passion. Yet what world was it?

The bedroom was lit up softly. She looked heavy in her eyes, as she lay there, suffused with the physical fire. She moved slowly in her white gown that fitted tightly. Her body was good, positive, extending a healthy warmth, because she really wanted him. There was no clammy self-restriction about her, like a lizard or a fish. Now she wanted to lie close to him and talk. Only it wasn't romantic, or personal revelation: neither wanted this. They moved close together in the bed.

It was an experience complete in itself. The room was dim, remote. Afterwards she was laughing. "You must go back soon." She looked sad, suddenly. "I want to be divorced." But he knew she was bound up finally with the rich world. She could not do without it.

"Before I was married - I was a nurse. My husband, he kept asking and asking me to marry him. But I wouldn't let him touch me for a long time after the marriage."

"And now?"

"Now I must let him. But as little as possible. He can never touch my breasts - I don't let him." She hugged herself to ward off the remembered possibility. The man felt a strong sympathy for this tangled life. "And he will be back soon. I must cook for him - and his friend." She kissed him, warmly, and moved up closer to him. "I like you very much."

They went to the kitchen. He liked it here. Big trees

173

swung in the wind just outside the window. Here you were level with the topmost branches. Although it was dark, you knew the trees were there, by the heavy rustling of the branches. The snow gleamed below, in the reflected light of the room. He sat at the table, peacefully, as the girl prepared the food.

They knew there would be no final release for her. If she was divorced she would go back to live in Teheran, with her mother and sisters. Her life would run in narrow tracks. She would like, perhaps, to marry this younger man. But he didn't want to marry her. What would they do together? The sensual love was a world in itself. His own separate self, thoughtful, she could not reach. What was it that a woman wanted from a husband? Did she just want sensual gratification? Did she want someone to talk to, about her feelings? Or did she want most of all, the sense of emotional closeness, an affinity between her own feelings and those of the man?

He knew ultimately there wasn't such an affinity. She was a materialist, rich; he was against her social activities. Once, with her in a large store, he had had a sudden vision of a million people, working in factories, going home at nights to dingy homes, so that this store would be full of goods for her to covet and buy. And her husband was rich as he was because he had managed to harness part of such a system to his own purposes: he was an overlord. The guest had told her of his thought. She'd laughed, prettily. "You think too much." But he knew the gap between himself and her that the sensual contact couldn't resolve; she had no sense of general justice.

She was a kind, generous woman in other ways. Only, because she could not think, he could not marry her. He would be a mystery to her, in his ideas. And she would come to hate him for his differences. "Why make life awkward - enjoy yourself." But the illness and the bitterness below her exterior maintained form was the price of this belief. She had no further faith, to move on, to a new

174

emotional impulse. And so everything would founder, torn up on the stones of a particular, limited upbringing, a single class and cultural view. Her husband sought his own pleasures, inside a membrane that could not be broken by real empathy with anyone. She was not so far gone. But such a condition was also her parents', that of the Persian upper class.

The Englishman liked her very much. In her body she was close to him at least. The other distance couldn't be crossed. They could play games of conscious understanding, but no more.

It was time for him to go back. He was grateful; he loved her as a sensual comrade and a generous warm hearted woman. Physically, they had been to the same place. Only his thoughts isolated him from her. She left him at the airport. He must press on harder, find another solution.